Attāsia Legends
Valley of Mystics

DAVID JAMES

Attāsia Legends

Valley of Mystics

DAVID JAMES

For information contact;
Integrated Publishing
www.integratedpublishing.press

Book design by Integrated Publishing
Cover design by David James, Azante Zamyslov & Gelb Paltov

ISBN: 978-0-6489601-1-9
First Edition: November 2022

10 9 8 7 6 5 4 3 2 1

Many thanks and gratitude to those whom without, this story would have remained nothing more than a dream.

CONTENTS

CONTENTS

PROLOGUE

Again with the dream. The night my mother died. Strange, how the memories of such a small child can remain as if they happened only yesterday. The sounds of the calming ocean sweeping across the deck of a large voyager ship bound for new land; the chance for a new life, the glimmer of the ocean as it reflects the last of the light from the sun before it dips beyond the horizon. These are far from whole memories. Just snapshots of images, feelings, smells, sounds.

I wonder sometimes if the face I see as my mothers' is really hers or something my subconscious invented. As much as I fear the dream, I find it something I yearn for. The pain of recalling such sadness seems to be outweighed by the amusement of the pure happiness felt when sensing the touch of the one who gave you the gift of being part of this world.

I too recall the fear. A force like a dark wave penetrating the core. The fear of loss, of sudden change, it all still feels so real.

The sun shone especially bright and the commotion surrounding the docks of Evelan was exciting for the young boy as his mother lead him up the ship's ramp. He had never seen a ship before and his mother seemed to be glad that they were boarding this one.

Evelan had always been the boy's home though, and until this very morning he hadn't ever given much thought to what may lay beyond. It was the place of his birth; where he had learned the ways of being a young boy and where he had taken his first steps. He had often enjoyed the strolls he and his mother would take along the banks of the river backing onto their home. It was like a new adventure every day. The green of the trees, the sounds of nature at its purest and the smell of the fresh morning dew were all things that he would miss.

The ship that towered in front of them now had a strange smell and reminded the boy of a time when his mother took him to see his grandfather. The boy's grandfather and his belongings had an odd mixture of smells. Oak, dust and the ocean; all smells of grand adventure. The wind blowing through the sails almost pleaded for the ship to leave the dock and it seemed everybody on board was also eagerly awaiting departure. As they set sail the boy and his mother were lead down a hallway to a cabin where their baggage cases had been taken. The boy's mother leaned down, taking a necklace from one of the bags and placed it around her son's neck.

"Your grandfather would be proud of you…of both of us. He loved to travel and now, we're going on our own adventure," she said as she scooped him into her arms and carried the two-year-old boy toward the deck.

Reaching the end of the hallway, the wooden doors were opened from the other side by a man dressed in white. The man took his white hat from his head and began twirling it in his hands, drawing the attention of the young boy. He stretched out his tiny arms to grab it, stopping short mid-reach. The boy was surprised by the man's features. He had never seen so much grey, fuzzy hair hanging from somebody's chin.

The man stood for a while talking with his mother when she smiled, nodding her head. The boy looked up at his mother and she smiled back down into his wide, blue eyes.

"The nice Captain is going to show us around his ship Derik," she said, turning to follow the Captain out onto the deck.

The ship was the biggest thing Derik had ever seen and seemed to go on forever. Exhausted from the tour Derik leaned his head over his mother's shoulder as the sun fell into the ocean. The Captain lead the two back to the deck of the ship, waving to the young boy as he walked away.

Derik looked up into his mother's eyes and blinked a few tired-tears away, turning his head to join her longing stare out into the seamless horizon.

The woman reached down to straighten the glowing blue stone necklace that hung from her boy's neck, flooded with memories of her own childhood.

"Your grandfather was a wise man… humph, 'the traveller' they would call him. He gave me this stone after returning from one of his grand trips. An island he said had a past those living there would rather forget. Altāsia I think he called it." She smiled as Derik yawned.

"I hope this stone brings luck to you as it has for me."

The last ray of light disappeared as she turned toward the ship's cabins.

"One day you will go on your own adventure and discover your path." The words whispered as softly as the sea's breeze. "You look exhausted, how about we call it a day.

"Hurry, Derik! Get up, something's happening... HURRY!" The panicked voice of the young woman came as she impatiently grabbed for Derik's hand. The room around them swayed savagely as the two stumbled toward the doorway. The beating sounds of a storm ravaged the night sky outside and a sense of terror flooded the cabin. A sharp shift moved the floor out from beneath their feet and Derik felt his mother's hand slip away as she was thrown into the wall. Rain flooded the cabin floor and through a bright and fleeting flash of light Derik could see the port window had been blown open.

Everything was so dark that Derik struggled to understand what was happening and began to scream. The woman scrambled to her feet and rushed towards her screaming boy.

"Derik, where are you? Mummy's right here."

A short sense of relief came across the mother as her hand touched the little boy's arm. She quickly scooped him up and crashed through the remains to the door of the cabin that was merely hanging from its hinges.

The dark hallways echoed with screams of panic from others on the ship and the thundering sounds of the storm outside.

As the two reached the door to the deck, the woman turned to see a great bolt of lightning explode away the hallway and cabins behind her, throwing the mother and child onto the crumbling floorboards.

The young boy quickly got to his feet and franticly waddled to where his mother lay motionless on the deck of a ship that was now sinking into a wild ocean.

The boy began to gently shake his mother, the hard drops from above stinging his arms and neck as the sea swelled over the sides of the ship.

His hands pushed on her soggy shirt and he began to cry as he realised she wasn't waking.

The rumble of another wave hitting the ship swept Derik onto his back. He clambered to his feet, his eyes searching for his mother in desperation. Squinting through tears and the drenching rain he saw a large shadowed figure scuttling toward him from within the cabin debris and two strong, hard hands reached down pulling him into unfamiliar arms.

The face with fuzzy hair that he was looking into he had seen earlier when he and his mother were shown around the ship.

"Derik, I don't think we're going to make ..." The Captain's sentence was cut short as he and Derik were tossed overboard by a large wave that swept across the deck. Floating for a moment Derik saw the remains of a ship in flame, debris tossed along the water's surface. He thrashed his arms and legs desperately trying to keep afloat.

The sea was brutal, swelling around the young boy as he plummeted into the dark depths of the ocean.

CHAPTER 1
THE LUNA ECLIPSE

As the sun rose above the hill tops surrounding Lūnam, Derik sat in his usual spot at that time of morning, on the branch of the biggest willow tree overlooking the cove, watching as what has been home to him for the past sixteen years began to come alive.

But something was different about today; Derik could almost feel it in the air, for today was the day of 'The Ritual.'

Derik reached for the pack lying by his side and removed the Lūnai Flute, known for producing a sound like that of a fine-tuned choir drifting through a gentle breeze and when played true creates a most spectacular show of lights that dance around the performer.

Bringing it to his lips, Derik softly breathed a beautiful melody of lights into the air, playing the flute to the rising sun as its light licked over the cove; a welcoming warmth beginning to flood the city below. The flute's majestic sound and light show floated around Derik's head, forming into a hologram that duplicated the scene of the sun rising above the cove in front of him.

By the time Derik got back to the village it was buzzing with excitement. People he knew, friends and neighbours were filling the streets, setting up stalls and already plopping themselves in the best position to view the festival.

As he did every two years that the festival arose, Derik made his way to the centre of the village, where stood one of the greatest monuments of his land and the cause for excitement.

He looked up at the great stone, triangular prism that reached into the sky almost beyond his sight range. The glyphs lining the sides were almost in position and all but one glowed a brilliant blue. Taking a small spyglass from the side of his belt, he looked to the top point of the prism. Hovering above the tip was one of the greatest mysteries of the land, The Orb of Asimēre.

The sunlight reflecting through the orb gave off a spectacular glow, but could not penetrate the red circular clouding cloaking the centre of the orb.

"Derik, there you are! I've been searching all over for you." A wise, crackly voice came from behind Derik.

Putting away his spyglass, he turned to see the shadowed face of a smaller man cloaked in a brown shawl.

"Ranūl, today's the day." Derik replied smiling from ear to ear.

"Yes Derik. Best we not forget to prepare for tonight." Ranūl crackled, gesturing for Derik to walk with him.

"How could I forget? Not only is this my favourite part of the twin-year but it's the last time I will be helping you before I take my journey around Altāsia."

"Ah, yes. The journey begins tonight. I almost forgot. It seems like just yesterday when you arrived. Hah. I remember the night clearly boy." Ranūl began the story Derik had come to know quite well.

"Exactly sixteen years ago. You were only two then. The waters of the ocean had already enclosed around the city and I was checking on the Luna Triad and the Orb. A great crashing sound rippled through the waters above and I knew it had to be a ship. It had been a while since we had seen a ship in these waters, but through my lifetime these treacherous waters have taken more than enough lives."

Ranūl paused for a moment, seeing the pain on Derik's face as he too remembered clearly the accident that claimed his mother's life.

"Shall I go on?" Ranūl raised an eyebrow in caution.

"It's alright Ranūl. Continue." Derik gestured, wiping the tears that had began to well in his eyes.

"Well, if I remember correctly, it was then that I saw a faint blue light in the water above the village. It was only small. So I followed 'til it came through the protective dome, shielding the village from the wild waters that surround it at that time of year." Ranūl paused again, as he knew that this was Derik's favourite part of the tale. He stopped walking and prepared himself to re-enact the moment he caught two-year-old Derik in his arms. He began with a funny little wobble followed by a few side steps and as though he was actually in that moment of time again, Ranūl fell to the ground mimicking the catch that saved little Derik's life.

Derik began to laugh at the thought of his tiny body 'crushing' Ranūl and reached out a hand to help him off the ground.

"I can't imagine what would have happened to me if you weren't there Ranūl." Derik said as they continued to walk through the crowds of people gathering around the prism, staring up at the glowing orb.

"Indeed...however, if it weren't for that blue stone you have around your neck," Ranūl gestured to the stone hanging from a chain that sat neatly above Derik's shirt-line, "You wouldn't have been able to pass through the dome at all."

Derik wrapped his fingers around the only object he had left that reminded him of a life long passed.

"Well. Best we get ourselves home Derik." Ranūl broke the silence.

Derik turned sharply on his feet toward their cabin, forcing a smile that he hoped would disrupt his grief and bounced off the chest of a tall burly man he hadn't noticed standing behind them.

"Oh, flumbar! I'm so sorry, I should have been watching where I was going."

"Nah, Don't worry about it, I barely felt you."

Derik's cheeks glowed a bright red and he again apologised, taking another step toward the cabin and stopping short when he heard Ranūl ask the man, a stranger to the village, who he was.

"My name is Sintar. I am from Castrene City at the centre of Altāsia. I have been travelling the island for a few months now and came across this little village only a few hours ago. What is with all of the festivities, are you having a celebration?"

Ranūl frowned and then smiled. "Oohh, somebody that doesn't know the history of Lūnam. Well sir let me enlighten you."

"Ranūl. I don't think this guy, Sintar was it, has the time to be listening to one of your tales." Derik said, gesturing for Sintar to make his move.

"Actually, quite the opposite. I would love to hear the history behind this little village." Sintar replied, taking a seat on a stump by the path.

"Derik. Sometimes it is better to listen. You never know; what it is that you may learn just might help you through your journeys." Ranūl replied turning back to Sintar with a grin and beginning the tale of Lūnam's past.

"Just beyond one hundred and twenty years ago this land was under siege by a great evil. Her name was Elanore and she had a need for vengeance. She had been born into the life of an enchanter and she had been shunned by the people of her city and cast out into the outskirts of the forest. Elanore was encompassed with revenge and so she felt she had no choice but to destroy all who would not accept her. She began taking the land with her army of mystics by her side and seized every city, village and town, destroying any of whom got in her way. My race of peoples, were also powerful, but not powerful enough to stop her."

In realising this was not going to be a short tale, Sintar bent his legs and sat cross-legged, his gaze eagerly fixed on Ranūl. "My apologies Ranūl. I have travelled quite a distance but please go on."

Without battering an eyelid, Ranūl's glimpse into the past was continued with a smile. "Although we tried, we failed. And thus we moved to this village. The furthest from the point she had made her lair. It was but two weeks before we learned perhaps this was not the best place to prepare ourselves for her impending assault. The two moons of Tellūs aligned and the forces generated pulled the ocean into the cove and drowned everyone. I had been chosen to be on guard at the hill tops surrounding the cove and watched as all of my family and friends lost their lives. It took me some time before I gathered strength, and to pay homage to my family lost, I needed to find a way to make this area of Altāsia secure."

Ranūl paused briefly, his eyes glazed as he recalled the memories of those he had lost.

"Though. There was a legend of an orb that had been passed down through my people's generations, the Orb of Asimēre. It had been formed by my people many moons ago to protect an island just off shore from here. One of the orb's capabilities could allow me to utilise the pull of the moons to create a protective dome that shielded its surrounds from the sea. I went in search of the orb and after a few months I found the mountain strewn island on which it was kept. The temple surrounding the mountains that held the island's triad was in ruins. I found the orb hidden beneath a collapsed wall, so I took it. I returned home and created the triad in the centre of this village to allow me to keep track of exactly when the moons would align, and then utilising the power of the two moons the orb and triad would create a barrier around the village to protect it from the treacherous waters."

"What a story!" Sintar replied, leaning in to listen closely to the what happened when Elanore arrived at the newly protected cove.

"Alas, Elanore was defeated before she reached this part of the island," Ranūl's disappointment showed in his tone. "I never received the chance to avenge those that were lost, and although at first it felt as though my efforts were in vein, Altāsians began learning of this place and its powers to protect. A few moved here to begin their lives again after the carnage that Elanore bestowed upon this land and now every two years, when the moons align, I must perform the ritual to use the powers of the moons to protect all that dwell here."

Sintar sat in awe before words escaped his lips. "Whoa. So you're over one hundred and twenty years old. Amazing!"

"Our race lives to be over two hundred and fifty years young sir and until I find another to take my place and perform the protective ritual I cannot, shall not, pass into the next realm."

"Well, this is something we didn't learn in the history books. Thanks for the lesson, Ranūl was it?" Sintar said, pushing on the ground to get to his feet and reaching out to shake Ranūl's hand.

"I think I might go find myself a place to bunk though. I would love to experience being here while the village is underwater. I will see you later," Sintar said as he walked into the crowds to observe the Orb of Asimēre.

Ranūl turned to Derik and pointed his hand toward the direction of their cabin and the two continued.

"He seemed enthralled by that story Ranūl." Derik said as they approached the cabin door.

"Well Derik, not all have heard the true story of Altāsia's past. Perhaps one day you will learn more than I know and I can count on you to take my place as the village protector." Ranūl said, placing his hand behind Derik's shoulders and pushing him gently up the cabin's steps.

As they entered a small cabin at the edge of the village Derik stopped, remembering there were still a few items he needed for his journey.

"I just have a few final errands to run before we prepare for the eclipse." Derik called to Ranūl heading back toward the village. Ranūl returned the wave and entered the cabin they called home.

By the time Derik returned Ranūl was adorned in his white ceremonial robes.

"Derik, you're just in time," he said through a smile.

"If you wouldn't mind assisting me, I need some freshly ground Luna stone for the ... Oh what do you have there?" Ranūl paused as he noticed that Derik was holding a small round package.

"It's nothing really. I just thought ... I leave for my journey soon and I wanted to get you something, for all you've done for me." Derik replied, handing the package to Ranūl.

A little surprised, Ranūl picked up the small package and began to tear the wrapping, revealing a small emerald green sphere.

"Where ever did you get this?" Ranūl asked in disbelief, "I've been searching for one almost my entire life, they're impossible to come by and incredibly powerful. You know this stone allows the beholder to breathe underwater?"

Derik, holding his head high, simply smiled back and replied, "Of course I know, and I have my ways of finding what I want."

"Oooohh, you and your cheek; I've always said it is a lure to unwanted troubles," Ranūl chuckled.

"Well so long as we are in the giving mood, I do have a few things for you Derik."

Ranūl walked over to his ritual cupboard and took from the top shelf a small bottle and square package wrapped in parchment.

"I have been saving these for the right moment in time, and I am quite sure that now is that moment," Ranūl explained as he handed the items to Derik.

Derik turned his attention to the first gift. He carefully opened the slightly tattered wrapping to reveal a book. The title of the book was worn but Derik could just make it out. "Legendary Valley of Mystics," he read aloud, "Ranūl, what is this?" Derik asked in awe of its seemingly ancient look.

"Ah Derik, I forget how young you are, and how old I am," Ranūl chuckled. "This book is filled with tales from the ancients. It tells of Altāsian history, including the true story of this great land's history," he added, a vibe of honour quivering in his voice.

Derik slowly brushed his hand over the cover of the book, an eagerness to begin reading almost distracting him from the small bottle filled with clear liquid Ranūl had placed on the table.

"And what's in this bottle?" Derik asked lifting it curiously from the table.

That is to be used only in the most dire of situations and must not be wasted. They are tears from the Phoenix of Fire Mountains," he explained in the deep wise voice Derik knew all too well.

"But one drop will heal almost any wound! There are tales of this being used even to heal the recently deceased." Ranūl added placing a small piece of Luna stone into a mortar and handing it to Derik.

"Well, best not sit around here when there are preparations to be done." Ranūl said as matter of fact, bringing the conversation back to the preparations, before pausing once more and turning to Derik, eyebrows raised with curiosity.

"Have you your map of Altāsia?" he asked.

"It's in my pack." Derik replied looking over to his bed where a small woven pack lay in a heap.

"If north is where you travel first, the most grand of sights you will find," Ranūl crackled leaning back and taking a dusty book from the shelves behind him, opening to a page with a spectacular view of a waterfall.

"Waterfall Valley acquired its name due to the immense size of the falls," Ranūl explained. "But these images do not do it justice."

The thought of a grand waterfall as the first step in his journey sent shivers of excitement through Derik's body as he began crushing the stone Ranūl had passed him into a fine powder.

It was late afternoon when Derik and Ranūl arrived at the Luna Triad, and it seemed as though the entire village had now made their way to centre of the village. Fire breathers were performing daring acts to Derik's left and a group of children playing with sparkle sticks, chased one another through the crowds.

"It's time," Ranūl said as he gestured for everyone to step back. Derik took a step toward Ranūl and wrapped his arms around him.

"Then it is time for me to go," he said pulling away. "I'm going to miss you Ranūl."

"Indeed Derik. Take care," Ranūl replied with a smile, turning to again face the triad.

The beginning of the ritual was always a spectacular sight and Derik was disappointed that he was going to miss it this time. As he reached the top of the mountains surrounding the cove, the final rays of light fell behind the mountains shrouding the village in shadow.

"Ranūl should have sifted the Luna rock around the triad by now," Derik said to himself, wishing he was closer to see the final glyph move into place as Ranūl chanted the last word of the mantra that would create the protective dome around the village, while it was engulfed by the waters of the ocean.

Derik looked to the stars, watching as the two moons of his world began to meld into one. The very moment only one moon could be seen in the night sky Derik's attention fell back to the village centre and he waited with anticipation. Although it was a scene he had seen many times before, the great beam of light that then shot from the moon striking the Orb of Asimēre left Derik in awe. Beams of moonlight echoed through the orb, shooting in all directions, beginning to circle around the village.

The sight was impressive from the mountain tops and as the beams combined to form the dome around Lūnam, Derik couldn't help but feel unsettled knowing that before dawn, Lūnam Village and all the people he cared about will be bound by the sea.

CHAPTER 2
WATERFALL VALLEY

It was hard for Derik to imagine being so far from home and the thought of Ranūl alone in a village that was now in its last day of being underwater was still worrying. It would only be so that something would go wrong whilst he was away.

Derik began to consider turning back when the sight that lay before him as he reached the edge of a grand valley brought to mind the reason for his voyage.

He stopped for a moment, rubbing his eyes in disbelief.

"Ranūl was right! The pictures don't compare," Derik whispered to himself.

The valley that lay before him looked like it had once been home to a great forest, but now only few trees remained to the west of a grand city that lined the centre. It was odd how the greenery of Altāsia seemed more vivid than the images he recalled from the fading memories of a place he and his mother once called home.

There were so many things to take in all at once, but Derik's attention had been focused on the magnificent waterfall the village was renowned for; the Gigas Falls. Vast amounts of water flowed from within the left side of the mountains surrounding the luscious valley, pouring over a cliff face which had been carved into the mountains over millions of years, and even from a distance the water shimmered a brilliant blue.

Reaching the entrance to the village he continued under an impressive oak sign that stretched the road.

"Waterfall Valley; Platoda Road." Derik read aloud, "What an entrance!"

Derik stood immersed in a bustling city much different from his home.

To his left, the store closest to him was offering handmade furniture. Halflings, Light Workers, and all types of other people from across the land were hurrying in and out of the doorway, an identical scene lining the street on either side of the road.

Derik was taken back at the number of different stores; carpenter, repairs, even a theatre on the corner with a line that extended around the block. The hustle and bustle was so very different from Lūnam and Derik again began to feel homesick. He looked down at the gravel-paved road beneath his feet and kicked a stone which flew off to his left, hitting a man in the shoulder. The man looked to be in his mid-thirties, with grey-brown hair balding at the top and a measuring tape hanging from the pocket of his white overalls.

Derik winced. '*Flumbar*' he thought, '*You always go managing to find trouble, don't you?*' He smiled apologetically to the man and lowered his head.

"Oh! I'm sorry, I didn't mean it.""No, that's fine; I hardly felt it at all. The name's Drake, I'm the carpenter here in Waterfall Valley," the man replied in a hard and husky voice.

"I'm Derik, and sorry again about the stone."

"You're not from the Valley, are you?" Drake said as more of a statement than a question.

"Am I that obvious?" Derik replied rolling his eyes at the thought of being the centre of attention.

"Well you do stand out a little, and you have been standing in that same spot for a quarter of an hour now."

A large rumble interrupted the conversation and Derik reached down clutching his stomach.

"Urgh, I'm starving! Is there somewhere close by I could grab a bite and settle in for the night?" Derik asked, his face glowing a slight pink as another loud grumble interrupted.

Drake stopped for a moment, a look of concentration on his face.

"Now let me see, if you're after some tucker and a place to rest, you could check in at the Metaprep."

"The what...?" Derik asked, upon never hearing such a stranger name.

"The Metaprep. It's a lodge on top of a small restaurant. Mandan owns the place. Nice guy, he should look after you."

"Where would I find this Metaprep?" Derik asked, looking at his surroundings in desperation as another grumble escaped from his stomach.

"It's down by the Shifting Sands Bar toward the end of Woration Lane." Drake then pointed to a lane to his right.

"Great, I'll go and speak with, Mandan was it? Thanks for the help Drake," Derik replied with a smile and headed off to find himself some lunch and a soft bed to lay in.

As he neared the lane a small sign in the road became visible, 'Woration Lane'.

"This is it," he mumbled to himself.

The deeper into the laneway Derik walked, a strong feeling of uneasiness began creeping its way into the pit of his stomach as he noticed it consisted of mostly shadowed stores, and small groups of people standing around muttering things to each other as he walked past.

When he arrived at the front of the only building in the lane that still seemed to be in use, with a rather large sign with the letters T and P not quite visible, he pushed on the old red-wood doors and was hit with a waft of delight.

Inside was warm with light and the smell of amazing foods tickled Derik's senses. The bar was almost as busy as the streets and Derik wondered if he would even get a table.

To his left a group of rough looking Halflings were disputing one of their hands in a game of cards. On the other side of the room a rather tall man was seated at the far side of the tavern, alone. He had a moustache and very little hair, a long coal-black overcoat which draped down over his seat, and was peering into a little black box on the table in front of him.

Another wave of deliciousness drifted past Derik's nose and he turned his attention to the bar at the centre of the room, heading over to where a young man in a blue and white-chequered shirt stood drying a glass.

"Good day Mister, and what may I help you with?" enquired the bartender.

"I'm looking for a place to stay and something to eat. The carpenter told me I should speak with a ... Mandan." Derik explained.

"Well, you've definitely come to the right place, and you are?"

"Derik." Derik looked at the bartender's badge and saw that the name printed was Mandan. Derik reached across the bar and shook his hand.

"I'm headed on a journey around Altāsia and finishing up in the Valley of Mystics."

"The Valley of Mystics huh! I hear it is a very dangerous route to get there!" Mandan replied slightly shocked that such a young person would take on such a feat.

"Yes, I know, it's kinda one of the reasons I want to go, I love the thought of the challenge and adventure."

"Well as a matter of fact, you see that man sitting over there?"

Mandan then pointed at the tall, thin man Derik had noticed when he walked in.

"He is also going to the Valley of Mystics. But I would steer clear of him; darkness shadows his soul."

Wondering how Mandan might know this Derik stood with a twisted and confused look on his face until Mandan noticed this obviously needed further explanation.

"There have been tales of this man floating around the city since his arrival two days ago. He is in search of a group of roughians to accompany him. Those who have spoken to him say he has been muttering on about a release of the grandest of powers and ideals about ruling the world alongside his 'queen.' He asked to stay here whilst he was in search of 'followers' and, well, business is business so I obliged. But seems like a nut case to me, I would stay away from him just in case."

"Oh…thank you," Derik replied thinking Mandan's caution was a little odd. "Do you have any idea what's in that little black box he has on the table in front of him?"

Mandan looked over to the man, back to Derik and with a confused look on his face replied, "I have no idea, but he's been staring into that thing for at least an hour now, with the same crazed expression on his face. Now on to more important matters, what can I get you for lunch Derik?"

Looking up at the rather large board above the bar, Derik was surprised at some of the meal names.

"Eye of Water-lizard with Local Greens and Beaten Beast what...?" Derik looked back to Mandan with an eyebrow raised.

"Hmmm, what's the Sea Serpent Skin like?" he asked

"It's a very tasty meal and comes with a side dish of Brasen Beast-horn Soup."

Derik recoiled at the thought and decided to stick with a glass of water and a piece of Marland Bread.

"Alright, when you come back down I will have lunch ready for you."

Mandan then reached behind the counter and produced a small silver key.

"Here's the key to room number seven. Just head up the stairs and it's on the left."

With that in mind Derik took the key and headed for the stairs, all the time his gaze fixed on the hunched over man and his box. As Derik passed he slowed his pace to see if he could steal a look at what was within, his curiosity eating at him from the pit of his stomach.

Coming to a stop when he was directly behind, he got to his tip-toes and peered over the seats. Inside, the box contained a small white pendant depicting a Mystic holding what seemed to be half a deep black stone with green markings etched into it. Derik traced the lines of each image in his mind, trying to make sense of them;

To Derik's surprise the markings were similar to those on the Luna Triad back home and was in deep thought when the man sharply turned and glared into Derik's eyes. Caught by surprise Derik tripped over his feet, quickly regained his balance and hastened up the stairs to room number seven.

Derik closed the door silently, wondering if he should have taken Mandan's warning a little more seriously. He walked over to the bed and placed his pack down, reaching in and removing the Lūnai flute. To the right of the room a large window looking out at the falls beckoned. He walked over and leaned against the sill, gently breathing out a soothing lullaby while plumes of light danced around the window.

Derik lowered the Lūnai after the final note and turned back toward the bed a little too sharply, kicking his shin into a small chest of drawers against the wall and sending the bottom drawer front sliding across the room. Rubbing his shin in agony, he hopped over to the drawer front and picked it up putting it on top of the chest of drawers.

"I'll deal with you later," he said through gritted teeth to the motionless piece of wood.

Feeling a bruise already forming Derik waddled into the washroom to clean up for lunch. He peered into the mirror and a dirty face stared back, his sandy hair still parted at each side sitting at the length of his chin. The dirt on his face was covering his light tan, so it didn't bring out the colour of his deep blue eyes as it normally did.

He turned the tap of the basin and cupped a handful of water splashing it to his face, grabbed the towel on the wall rack and dried the water off. When he looked back in the mirror he was pleased with the sight of a clean face.

As Derik returned to the bar Mandan greeted him with a tray containing his Marland and a glass of water.

"Thank you," Derik said politely as he took his lunch.

"You're welcome," Mandan replied as he took the six silver coins that Derik gave in return for the meal.

Derik went to a table at the back of the Metaprep and sat down. While he ate his thoughts wandered back to the stone he had seen earlier. The markings were so odd and his curiosity got the better of him once again. Swallowing the last bite he headed out the doors and back toward the village centre.

Reaching Platoda Road he looked desperately up and down the now nearly vacant street. He had somewhere in mind but wasn't sure where he'd find it in such a large and unfamiliar city. He walked back toward the entrance to the village figuring he stood better chance starting from there. As he neared the entrance sign a familiar figure stepped out from the carpentry store, turned and slid keys into the keyhole to lock the doors.

"Drake," Derik called out, waving frantically to get the man's attention. Drake turned and jogged over to Derik in a hustle.

"Hello again, what can I help you with?" Drake said speedily.

"Hi Drake, sorry. Have I caught you at a bad time?" Derik replied noticing that Drake seemed a little impatient.

"Oh, no...Sorry Derik I've just had a long day. What can I do for you?"

"I'm looking for a library."

"Ah, yes that I can help with. The library is just over in that big white building," Drake replied, pointing toward a large majestic building a few blocks down the street.

Thanking Drake, Derik ran down the street but came to a halt as he reached the library, standing in awe of the monumental marble white structure in front of him. He took the first step, slowly walking the stairs and through doors that were four times as taller than the top of his head.

Stepping through the doorway, the inside reminded Derik of a chapel from one of Ranūl's books back home, with its grand pillars, but instead of pews it was lined with bookshelves that reached to the ceiling. In front of the doorway Derik noticed an empty desk with a silver bell that was begging to be rung. He walked over and tapped the button top. A loud ding echoed through the hallways of books and as the dying sound faded, a small woman with hair wrapped in a bun appeared out from behind one of the bookshelves.

"Hello dear," the woman said as she reached the front desk. "Is there anything I can help you with?"

Derik thought for a moment about the best way to ask for what he was trying to find.

"Umm? Do you have anything on languages and writings?" he asked.

The librarian simply nodded her head and beckoned for Derik to follow her, stopping at a section of the library that had many books that read 'Not for Loan' on their spines.

"Most of our books on language can be found in this area. If you need anything else, I won't be far away," the librarian said, leaving Derik to search and returning to sort through a trolley of books.

He pulled one of the books from the shelf and quickly but carefully scanned through it.

"Nope, nothing in here," Derik mumbled to himself, as he reached for another.

The pages of the next book were frail at the edges, the cover bound in dust and the title worn with age but Derik could still make it out.

'*Ancient Languages of the Ages, well if it's not in here then I don't know where I'll find it,*' Derik thought to himself as he opened the front hardcover of the book. He scanned the index and flicked to a page with the sub-heading Ancient Languages in Writing, searching the pages for the symbols. Turning the next page excitement swept through Derik when his eyes came across an image of three symbols that looked identical to ones he remembered from the stone.

He reached down and silently but swiftly tore the page from the book shoving it into his pocket and being sure he hadn't been seen, headed for the entrance and out the doors.

Once back in his room Derik took the page from his back pocket and sat on the bed reading intently. The page told of a once commonly used written language which possessed a great spirit and with the correct use could grant the beholder true power. The language of the Ancients. Derik reached the end of the description; which had only described the time the writings were used and it seemed, their forgotten past. Still left curious he folded the page. He jumped up from the bed to place the page in the chest of drawers and a gaping hole in the bottom caught his attention, reminding him of the broken drawer front.

"Well, I'd better get you back on or Mandan will have a fit I'm sure," Derik mumbled to the piece of wood. He reached down and slid the drawer from the base, took the front and gently knocked it back on. He took hold of the knob and pulled gently, sliding the base out and peering into the empty drawer, smiling at his newly found 'carpentry' skills. He again pushed gently to close the drawer and it didn't budge, his triumphant smile fading from his face. Giving it a harder shove the vibrations caused a small folded piece of parchment to fall from the bottom of the drawer above. He reached in lifting it out and unfolded the tattered page. The torn edges made it difficult to read.

"Temple Tempus, what or where is that?" Derik wondered aloud. Figuring it was nothing more than a lonely traveller's drawing he gently folded it back up and placed it on the bedside table. He leaned over and blew out the candle lighting the room from the darkness outside and lay down on his bed, closing his eyes. He lay in the dark. Every sound becoming amplified by the quiet and as he began to drift into sleep, a light thumping from the hallway caught his attention. The sound grew louder; thudding past his room and stopping close by. The quiet returned again for a few moments until interrupted by a light tap, followed by a creak. Concluding it was a visitor for the room next to his own he put his ear up to the wall and strained to hear the conversation, Ranūl's voice echoing through his mind '*Derik, one day your curiosity will get you into trouble*.' He could just make out the words reverberating through the wall and Derik couldn't believe what he was hearing.

"I just don't think I should risk it, we must do something," one of the muffled voices vibrated through the thin wall.

"I could have something arranged, but of course at a price," replied a second deeper toned voice.

"Arrange it. All the money on Tellūs won't matter if all goes to plan."

Derik then heard footsteps return to the other side of the room and the door once again squeaked open.

"I'll see that it goes to plan, and I will see you in the morning Xardos," the deeper voice said closing the door.

Once the thumping of footsteps could no longer be heard Derik laid his head back on his pillow, thinking of what he had just overheard and whether he should inform Mandan. After a few minutes of silence the day's travelling got the better of him and he drifted into sleep.

Shock still rippled through his body as Derik lay in a cold sweat staring up at the ceiling, images of the night terror he was all too familiar with still flashing through his mind.

Although it was a dream he had been having almost every night since he was two, it was still hard to readjust to being awake. He looked to his window and up at the stars, his thoughts taken back to his mother, when a shadowed figure passed by his window from within the room. He watched frozen with fright as it neared the bed, moving swiftly and silently. Panic began to overcome his still drenched body. As the figure moved to the edge of his bed, Derik remembered the candlestick on his bedside table and sprung into action grabbing the holder and thrusting it into the leg of the shadow. A deep loud scream boomed from his attacker as they stumbled backwards, giving Derik time to jump from the bed and dash out the door.

The streets outside looked different at night but strangely Derik felt more comfortable in the dark gloomy alley than in his room right now. He sat down at the entryway of the Metaprep and waited until the scampering of footsteps coming from inside came to a halt. Reluctantly, Derik mustered the courage to go back inside, and lighting a candle, quickly made his way back to his room. He pushed on the ajar door and peered inside to see a now empty room. He hastened toward the drawers removing his book on the Valley of Mystics and fearing that the assailant might attack again, wedged it underneath the door locking it from the inside.

Derik awoke with the sunlight pouring through the window and onto his face. He sluggishly got to his feet and wobbled into the washroom, cupping a handful of water and splashing it to his face to shake free from the drowsiness throbbing through his head. He turned to make his way downstairs to get some breakfast when he suddenly remembered the attack during the night.

Once downstairs he wondered if he should speak to Mandan but was there any point? He had no idea who it was in the room, nor why they were there so he simply ordered some toasted Marland, with a glass of water and sat down at the spot at the back of the room.

While he ate Derik pondered over who it might have been in his room last night when the group of Halflings playing cards in the tavern the day before walked down the stairs, alongside the tall dark man Mandan had warned him of. To Derik's surprise the tallest had his leg wrapped in a bandage.

Derik bit his lip, feeling his brow wrinkle with worry, the only thought running through his mind, to leave town.

He didn't want to stay at the Metaprep another night for fear of his life and headed to his room after breakfast, packing his belongings and walking downstairs to greet Mandan standing at the bar who was juggling a handful of empty plates.

"I really must move on. I have a long journey ahead of me. Thank-you for the room," Derik said as he reached out to help Mandan place the plates safely down.

"Not a problem Derik. Is everything alright? You look like you've seen a Mystic."

Derik paused for a moment, rethinking his previous thoughts as he looked over to the group standing around Xardos pointing in his direction, some raising their hands to their throats, their index finger striking a horizontal line.

"Mandan. I have something to tell you." Derik said, eyebrows raised in concern. "I was attacked last night in my room. Don't look please, but I am pretty sure it was the group standing over by the stairs with the man you said to stay clear of."

Mandan winked at Derik.

"No need to worry. You said you were ready to leave. Have you all your belongings?"

Derik reached down to his pack and tapped it. "Yes."

"Then leave this to me. I will give you time to get out of town. But..." Mandan paused, a little grin growing on his face. "Please do return."

Derik smiled and nodded, turning toward the door as Mandan stormed to the group, eyes blaring. "What is this I hear you smashed a window in my establishment last night. You simple party goers have no right. You WILL pay for that! All of you sit down right now." Derik herd Mandan's booming voice as he slunk out the door.

CHAPTER 3

FOREST OF NIGHT

As the sun glared down from above and the clear blue of the sky making for a perfect start to the early afternoon, Derik was reminded of his arrival in Waterfall Valley. He turned to look in the direction of where the great city would be, but had been walking for so long that it was no longer visible over the hilltops.

There were a lot of things on Derik's mind, he was thinking about the stone with the strange markings on it, why had someone tried to attack him, was the map he had found in the drawer at the Metaprep real?

He reached into his back pocket and removed the map, unfolding it to again try and make sense of its bearings. Looking over the markings Derik noticed a familiar name but couldn't make sense of why it would be so prominently marked on the tattered map.

"Hmmm! It says the entrance is found in the Forest of Night, Where have I seen that before?" Derik mumbled to himself.

Placing the map back into his pocket he took out the book Ranūl had given him and looked within the cover where the land of Altāsia was intricately printed. He briskly searched over the printed words and stopped short when his eyes flicked across the name he was looking for.

"Forest of Night, I knew I'd seen it before," Derik said smugly. From the directions shown on the map the forest lay just ahead and looking up from where he was standing, he noticed the tips of trees along the horizon ahead of him.

'*I can't see any harm in taking a day from my journey to see if there is any truth to this map.*' Derik thought, taking a seat by a large oak tree by the path.

"This may be the last time I see you for a while," Derik said looking at the sun, deciding to take advantage of its warming rays before heading into the dense, dark forest.

He lay down, plopping his head on his pack and stared up into a perfect blue sky, his eyes growing heavier and closing lightly.

Derik awoke to what felt like drops of ice falling onto his face. Darting to his feet he frantically searched for shelter, as the drizzle quickly became a downpour. His mind suddenly snapped back to complete consciousness and he remembered the forest just up ahead and ran toward the cover of the canopy.

The heavy rain pierced through Derik's shirt, stinging his skin and large drops flowed down his forehead, blurring his vision while he staggered for shelter.

Reaching the forest's edge he suddenly noticed the downpour was no longer hammering his body, although the blinding rain still drenched the earth beyond the edge of the forest. Catching his breath Derik looked up to where he expected to see spots of sky but the branches above were so thick it blocked the storm raging above.

He turned back to the gloomy insides of the forest. As his eyes adjusted to the dark, Derik could make out the shadowy innards through flashes of bright lightning and he took a few steps into the dark depths of the Forest of Night.

Wondering if he would ever see the sky in full again Derik took a seat on a fallen tree stump. He sat listening to the absolute silence surrounding him and wondered why anybody would want to venture into such a place, when a rustling noise close by interrupted his trail of thought.

He got to his feet and stared into the eerie forest, silence again flooding his ears.

"Hello? Is there somebody there?" Derik's quivering voice echoed through the darkness. He turned his head sharply, his eyes straining to see through the black when a blinding flash of light snatched away his vision sending him stumbling backward. As his sight quickly returned Derik found himself face-to-face with a colossal blue Mystic.

The resonating heat from the Mystic's breath wafted over Derik's face and the smell of rotting flesh was just as unappealing. The great creature outstretched its scaly wings. Standing high it towered over Derik, its jaws large enough to swallow him in one bite.

"Thi...This can't be happening. There are no Mystics left in Altāsia." The words fumbled from Derik's lips.

Derik attempted to lunge in the opposite direction, but his legs wouldn't budge leaving him frozen in place. The Mystic reared its head, a rumbling coming from deep within its throat. Derik found his feet and swiftly began darting through the trees, the forest whirling by him. Derik saw no point in slowing to see how close he was to becoming the Mystic's lunchtime snack, but the forest around him didn't seem to agree and a long hard object beneath his feet cracked dropping him to his knees. He clambered to his feet and swung around in time to see the Mystic rear its head and blow a giant ball of fire towards him.

He shut his eyes tightly, raising his arms in front of his face as if trying to shield himself from the inferno he knew was coming but instead of burning, Derik began to grow icy cold. Lowering his arms, he creaked open one eye and found himself standing alone on a frozen lake top. Standing silently and in a panic, confusion began creeping across Derik's face as he realised the Mystic was nowhere to be seen. He took a step back toward the lake's edge stopping short as a deep crack boomed from the ice beneath. The frozen top gave way under his weight, plunging Derik into the icy water.

The lake's innards were chilling to his bones and the longer he was underwater the harder Derik found it to move. Kicking ferociously he broke through the surface clutching at the air, searching for something to grab hold of when he felt his hand come into contact with another, pulling him free from the icy water and quickly dragging him to the shore.

Catching his breath he lifted his head to thank the person who had saved his life and was surprised to see a shadowy figure cloaked in a long black shawl, disappearing into the forest.

Shivers ran through Derik's body while he sat dripping in ice cold water. Stumbling to his feet he turned to find himself at the steps to an old log cabin awkwardly perched by the lake's edge. Derik waddled onto the porch and knocked on the door. No answer.

He reached out and turned the dust covered handle pushing the door ajar.

"Huh...p-perrrffect, lookss l-l-like no-one's be-e-een here for a while." Derik stuttered, noticing a great hole through one of the walls at the back of the cabin.

Grabbing a few pieces of broken timber from the floor he looked around the room for something to ignite the wood. He walked over to the fireplace and threw the wood at the charred remains, knocking a small glass bottle just out from beneath the ashes.

Derik leaned down and picked it up, rolling the bottle in his hand. The label was faded and he thought it best not to bother with it, and tossed it back into the fireplace. The bottle smashed as it came in contact with the wood and bright orange flames leaped from the bottle's remains, enveloping the fireplace and setting the planks alight.

Sitting in amazement Derik huddled closer to the flames thankful of his luck, the warmth beginning to thaw his shuddering body.

Turning to dry his back he now saw the room flooded in light and a familiar sense washed over Derik, giving him the oddest feeling he had been there before. A small cupboard hung on the wall opposite the fireplace and Derik felt compelled to look inside.

He got up from the floor and pulled on the small rickety handle revealing three shelves filled with small bottles.

"*Incendium, Protectied, Luminesce* ... they sound like names of potions Ranūl would keep in his cupboards," Derik said realising he must be standing in an old enchanter's cabin. Taking the bottles and putting them in his backpack, Derik searched the cabin one last time for anything useful before snuffing out the fire and continuing through the forest.

The silence somehow seemed eerier than before as Derik inched cautiously through the forest. The thought of the warming sunlight on his face kept Derik pushing on when a ringing hiss broke through the quiet. Derik froze listening as the hiss echoed through the trees from all directions. He took a step forward and squinted through the night-like darkness of the forest and as quickly as the strange noise had begun, it ceased, silence again returning to his surrounds. Taking a few more steps forward Derik stopped short as the hissing again broke through the dark. Backing away from the direction of the now almost deafening noise Derik's foot hit a tree root sending him crashing to the forest floor, where he found himself staring into the eyes of a giant hairy eight-legged beast.

Terror pumped through his veins and his head began to feel light. He grabbed desperately at the earth, trying to drag himself away when a shooting pain ripped through his right thigh. The incredible heat sent Derik into shock as his sight began to dissolve into complete darkness.

He wasn't too sure how long he had been unconscious for and through a splitting headache Derik's eyes slowly creaked open. The hard rock face was rough against his back and the blinding darkness didn't help the nauseous feeling in Derik's stomach as he slowly came to. Struggling with what strength he had left he lifted his arms and tried to get up, soon remembering the excruciating pain throbbing in his thigh. He reached down to feel the wound but instead of flesh his hand came into contact with a sticky substance that was wrapped around his waist, holding him to the rocky surface. It seemed the more he struggled, the tighter it bound him to the rocks and he could feel his body growing weaker with every pull.

Straining to see through the deep black, Derik reached an arm out in front of him and quickly recoiled as his hand brushed past a thick coat of wirelike hair. A familiar piercing hiss sent chills down his spine and he began to struggle erratically when the substance holding him down finally broke free. Derik wasn't sure if it was just the spider venom coursing through his blood, but he felt as though he was sliding across the floor and soon began to realise he was not sliding across, but downward off a wall. Falling deep into the earth he dreadfully awaited the thump of hitting the ground.

CHAPTER 4
AETAS SWORD

The throbbing pain turning to numbness allowed him to draw no more than short shallow breaths, and a ghastly thought dawned on Derik as he lay dying. Not knowing where he was could only mean that nobody else did either and all hope of being saved faded from his mind.

The events over the past couple of weeks flooded into Derik's mind and he couldn't help but wish he had returned home after the attack in Waterfall Valley. He opened his eyes and lifted his chin slightly from the floor and a small stream of light from above let him see a small shadowy heap lying in front of him. He slowly dragged his arm along the sandy floor and reached out, grabbing the soft mound and dragging it to him. Opening the latch to his pack he reached in and slowly sifted through the inside when his fingers touched a small glass object. Derik removed the small bottle from his pack, holding it close to his eyes. The deep darkness made it difficult to see but a tiny stream of light from above was enough to make out the label.

"*Salūbris*. Well, it couldn't hurt," Derik thought hoping that the tales of enchanters being known for their healing held truth. He popped the small cork from the bottle and tipped the contents into his mouth. The brew stung as it dribbled into his stomach and a sudden drowsiness flooded Derik's body. He closed his eyes and embraced the impending darkness.

As Derik's eyes wearily opened, he no longer felt pain. The substance in the bottle had worked and now a feeling close to having the most restful sleep of his life flooded in waves through his body. Derik pushed on the floor beneath him and lifted himself from the ground, brushing the dust from his shirt and light unexpectedly filled the room around him. The sudden movement had triggered two lanterns hanging either side of the room to burst into flame, illuminating the rocky cavern he now found himself trapped in.

"Whoa, I have got to be one of the luckiest people alive! And lucky to be alive." Derik said aloud, his voice carrying through the underground chasm, echoing through the dimly lit tunnel to his left. He looked to the ceiling where a small ray of light was still filtering through the cracks of the now blocked tunnel he had fallen in from. The escape from the giant spider floated into Derik's mind and he shuddered at how close he came to death. He turned facing the seemingly deep tunnel and picked up his pack. He took a step and wobbled slightly, his legs still recovering from the fall, but quickly regained his balance. Derik began heading through the cave, a deep curiousness, and knowing that he could not, and did not want to, go back the way he came, pushing him forward. He walked to the wall nearby. Two iron doors, blocked his way forward.

"Flumbar! What do I do now? Derik's words of disappointment bounced off the walls, a small trickle of sand falling from markings in the middle of the iron doors the result.

Derik took a step, wiping the dust covered etchings on the door into his shirt. Intrigue zipped through his mind as the letters were revealed.

"Temple Tempus!" His wondering words echoed back to him as the removal of dirt revealed the golden embossed words. He reached into his pack removing the map he had found earlier, unfolding it and staring at the entrance point of the Forest of Night, where he had fallen in. He looked at the map and back to the doors that lay before him.

"Oh, am I glad I found you," he said, the map reflecting the tunnel's system that lay ahead of him and back out to the surface.

Derik pushed. The rusted iron rough under his hands. A loud groan came from deep within the metal, but the doors didn't budge. He took a step back and feeling rather like a fool, noticed a large padlock hanging at the base of the door.

Filled with utter hopelessness Derik closed his eyes, his head falling to the left.

"Now what am I going to do? I'm never going to get out of here!" He said as he opened his eyes and slumped onto the doors, sliding to the floor. He turned to the left and furiously flicked a handful of sand on the floor into a heaped pile of bones. Derik leaned in closer, realising he hadn't noticed them as he had approached the doors. On either side of the doors lay two heaped mounds of bone scattered throughout piles of battle armour. Derik pushed on the hard sand floor to his feet and stepped to the pile closest, sifting through in search of something amongst the armour he could use to break the lock open. He lifted what looked like the headpiece and raised it to place it over his head when a human skull slipped out of the bottom and rolled across the floor.

Derik dropped the helmet and reached for his mouth, gagging as the thought of sifting through human remains dawned on him. He looked back toward the helmetless pile of bones at his feet and noticed a small wooden board. The thought of going through the bones again didn't quite tickle his fancy but once again curiosity soon got the better of him and he closed his eyes as he reached over and picked up the wooden plank. He brushed the dirt from the face of the board revealing golden embossed writings inscribed deep in the wood.

'WE, THE GARDIANS OF THE GATE EXIST TO PROTECT AND SERVE OUR KING 'TILL OUR DEMISE. UNLESS THOU ART WORTHY, NO SOUL SHALL PASS.'

"Huh, over-protective bunch," Derik said throwing the sign to the floor. "Well, let's see what I can do about these doors."

Basic knowledge suggested he use something harder than the lock to smash it free from the doors. He picked up the empty helmet from the floor and walked to the doors, smashing it against the rusted padlock. The lock didn't budge.

"Urrgh." His disappointment reflecting his thoughts of having to once again sift through the piles of the dead. Derik reached into the bones, pulling out what he imagined would have been a femur of the guard and returned to the lock.

He wedged it inside the lock's ring, forcing hard toward the ground, the lock breaking in two and crashing to the floor. Derik pushed on the now security free doors and with a loud creak they opened oddly with ease.

As the doors swung slowly open the room inside lit up with firelight as again lanterns hanging on the walls burst into flame. Astonished and amazed Derik entered the temple's rather small entrance room. He reached into his pocket and removed the faded map of the temple hoping it was as real as the room he was now standing in. According to the readable pieces of the maze-like scribble on the page the door to his left would take him on the path to the other side of the temple, where Derik prayed to the Gods he would find a way out. He looked to the left of the room where there was an old wooden oak door. It seemed the map held some truth. He walked over and twisted the handle and just as before the room he entered lit up with firelight. A deep chasm fell in front of him, towers of stepping columns making their way across the room to the other side.

"This is going to be tricky." He whispered to himself, placing his hand on his pack to steady and taking the first leap. As he reached half way, he stopped, pulling the map close to his face.

"Ok, once I get through here, I need to make my way to the left." He said aloud, pointing hard at the map, the force knocking it from his fingers, floating down and away from reach into the chasm below. "Nooo!" His deafening cry echoed through the room as the map disappeared from sight. Head down in defeat, Derik jumped to the next column and then onto the ground before the exit door, turning back to the darkened abyss.

"Well. I guess I will have to wing it." The doors creaked open as he pushed to reveal a hallway with tunnels leading left and right.

"At least I know I have to go left." His voice echoed down the tunnel as he took his first step into the unknown.

After choosing doors at random, resting, snacking on his rations and then walking and choosing at random for what seemed like weeks, Derik stood in the centre of a square room with doors centred within each wall surrounding him. He had been relying on the faded map found in Waterfall Valley and he had no chance but to continue making decisions based on chance.

"Oh. Flumbar! Eeney, Meeney, Miney ..." The door to his right was chosen. He walked over and pulled on the rusted handle, opening it with ease and entered a room that was much larger than any other he had been in. A small stream of light cracked through the ceiling and reflected from a mirror, illuminating an unrolled scroll displayed on a stone podium in the middle of the room.

Derik walked over and picked it up but had a hard time making sense of the story he was reading.

"A sword named Aetas that has the ability to manipulate the time of nature?" Derik questioned aloud.

After reading a rather interesting tale that finished with a caution to the possessor of the Aetas Sword, warning to never let the beholder seize it without a brace, he placed the scroll back on the podium and as the weight of the scroll pushed on its stand, the floor began to shake. Small rocks and sand began falling from the roof above and the ground surrounding the podium cracked open. Dust filled the room as a larger podium rose from the floor, revealing an intricately woven sword bound in thin leather straps and a silver wristband adorned with a single red stone by its side.

Derik slowly reached for the sword and quickly recoiled, his fingertips feeling as though they were eroding from his bones to the tip of his skin. He leaned in reading the words inscribed on the sword and only one stood out, as he had just learned it from reading the scroll.

"Gladius Ex Aetas." He whispered the words aloud.

Suddenly the scroll began to make some sense and according to reason, Derik guessed he must be wearing the bracelet sitting by the sword in order to hold it, but doubt still swamped his mind as to why.

The bracelet felt cold against his skin but he liked the way it fit so snugly against his wrist.

'*Here goes nothing*' Derik thought as he reached again for the sword. The feeling of his fingertips eroding didn't persist this time and Derik picked up the sword, removing it from its sheath. It was well balanced as Derik swung it from side-to-side. He had always wanted his own sword but Ranūl had firmly educated him in the ways of harmony. He had often enjoyed training with the Swordsmith in Lūnam, albeit against Ranūl's knowledge, and considered himself an adequate swordsman at the very least.

Returning the sword back to its sheath Derik looped the strap over his shoulder and turned towards the only other door in the room.

The door closed as the room he had entered was littered with light. Once again, only a single door lay in front of Derik as he stepped forward into the large room. '*Well, this is another easy choice*' Derik thought. The white marble like rock of the door accentuated with the words 'BEWARE' etched into a panel by the handle. Derik shrugged his shoulders and turned the brass knob, cautiously entering the room.

At first the room lay in darkness but the temple's 'automatic' lighting brightened the walls before he could blink. Derik's attention was quickly drawn to the roof. He was astonished to see that it was made of not rock, similar to the rest of the cavern he had been walking through, but sand that appeared to be rising and falling like rolling ocean waves, defying all he had learned of gravity. With his eyes glued to the odd ceiling Derik took a step forward, his foot falling on small bones littering the floor that crunched under the weight of his body. He made his way to the other side of the room, plagued with wonder as to how the sand seemed to defy logic. Derik stopped short as a small stream of sand began trickling from the ceiling onto his head.

A large shadow moved in swift circles above him, flicking sprinkles of the golden sea like roof onto his face and pressure began building in his chest. A loud sneeze escaped from his mouth. He looked back to the shadow on the roof and was stunned to see it was no longer there. His steps now echoing slow motion, Derik crept further toward the door, dodging the broken pieces of bone beneath his feet. A grazing sound from behind him bounced from the room's walls as a large shadowy figure emerged from the sand, crashing to the floor between Derik and the exit to the room.

The spiny skin around its mouth quivered as the beast let out a high-pitched squeal. Through panic, it took Derik a moment to realise standing before him was a creature he had read about in a book as a child. They were known as the Ampharo and were considered extremely dangerous to all that cross their paths.Derik backed away slowly, but knowing he could end up trapped in the underground kingdom, or worse dead, he decided there was no use going back. He had to get through to the door on the other side. He quickly reached for the sword hanging from his back he'd found earlier and began to swing it hoping the warning swings would push the creature aside. The Ampharo backed away to dodge the blade, reared its body toward the roof and let out another loud screech.

Derik shuddered as the sound sent a chill down the back of his spine and began to frantically swing again.

The Ampharo quickly dodged and hopped to the side swinging its extended claws at Derik, deeply scratching his forearm.

Shock riddled through Derik's body and his legs gave way, the sword flinging from his grip and sliding across the floor leaving him completely defenseless.

The creature let off another piercing screech and leapt toward Derik, foam dripping from its mouth. Staring into the beast's eyes as it lunged toward him Derik snatched a bone-shard from the floor and plunged it deep into the creature's lower abdomen. The creature's reaction to the pain seemed to be Derik's friend.

The Ampharo fell backwards in agony, clawing at the piece of bone now bulging from its body and Derik saw this as an opportunity to retrieve his sword. Crawling as fast as he could across the floor, he swiftly took hold of the handle, turned towards the creature and drove the sword into its stomach.

Loud, bellowing cries both high and low from deep within the Ampharo's throat as it fell to its knees clutching at the gash. Derik watched in amazement as its body began to erode away from the wound outwards, until nothing more than a pile of dust remained on the floor.

Dropping the sword in shock Derik ran toward the door and turned the handle slamming it sharply behind him.

Once he was safe and the door was closed tight, he fell to his knees and ripped a small piece of his shirt holding it tightly to the deep gash on his arm to stop the bleeding.

Derik took his backpack off and frantically searched inside for the bottle of phoenix tears.

The touch of the small glass bottle that contained the fabled liquid of healing filling him with hope that this would not be the end.

He popped open the lid and let a few drops fall onto the wound, the gash healing before his eyes.

Derik was growing awfully thankful that Ranūl had gifted the phoenix tears to him.

Derik knew he had been down in the temple for over a month, as he reached in to remove the last of his rations. The rooms of the temple were all beginning to look alike and Derik wondered if he was ever going to see sunlight again. He walked into the next room chosen at random and as with all the others it was lit with a warm glow. As Derik approached the door opposite the one he used to enter, the lanterns in the room on the other side lit up, revealing an open doorway with shattered pieces of the oak door covering the floor. Stepping over the shattered remains he took a seat on one of the dust filled chairs plopping his face into his hands, tears of failure and defeat welling in his eyes.

"AArrhh!! Is there any way out of here??" Derik's voice bounced off the walls of the room and echoed back into his ears.

Frustration filled his body and he picked up one of the golden goblets that sat in front of him and threw it at the wall on the other side of the room. Small rocks crumbled from the ceiling and the walls, floor and ceiling began to shake. Derik had set off a chain reaction and it didn't seem the walls were going to hold the roof for much longer.

He shot to his feet and turned toward the doorway when his foot caught on the chair leg and hurtled him into the rocky wall, which slid open through the force to reveal a secret narrow passage. Derik shuffled inside as a boulder fell, narrowly missing his back and blocking him from returning to the collapsing ruins.

Shuffling his way through the cramped and dark tunnel hope of freedom from the underground prison he had endured for two months was a sight for sore eyes as a distant light reflected from the walls before him. He shuffled quickly as excitement grew. The light growing brighter and the walls widening.

The space grew wide enough for Derik to stand and as he stepped into the blinding light of day a wave of fresh air blew across his face.

Derik had never been so happy to see the sun. He'd finally found a way out of the temple and the cliff face looking out to luscious green hills before him was the most beautiful sight he had seen in over a month.

CHAPTER 5

THE DIARY OF ELISSA WILKINSON

The events that had taken place over the past months had left Derik yearning to be in the comfort of home, a crackling fire only adding to the desire to hear one of Ranūl's crazy yet insightful tales. The sun set in the west and Derik turned south toward the direction of home, inhaling a deep breath and releasing with a disappointed sigh.

"Home I go," he whispered as he took his first steps of defeat.

The sun now fully below the horizon Derik was considering stopping for the night when through the darkening haze of light a village rose into view from behind the hilltop in front of him. The thought of a nice warm bed, a filling meal and being among other people again brought Derik's spirits up a little and he quickened his pace.

As he neared the village something odd became apparent about the shadowy silhouetted buildings. Reaching the village edge a great sense of defeat washed over him when he saw not the lively nightlife he expected, but a city that lay in ruins.

He stood staring blankly at what must have once resembled an entrance sign, half barely hanging on one of the supporting posts and the other half on the ground by his feet. The markings etched into the sign were too damaged to make out and as he walked through the deserted village he couldn't help but feel as though he shouldn't be there.

'*I wonder what happened to this place!*' Derik thought as he peered through a gaping hole in the side of one of the buildings. The dust covered furniture was scattered around the room and what remained of the walls was a charred mess.

Derik turned and made his way to the remains of a water fountain that would be better described as a rubble of stones. He stood looking around at a village which resembled the battle ground of a great war. Most of the building's walls were strewed over pathways, roofs missing and the tattered remnants of the resident's belongings scattered across the ground.

The silence was eerie and Derik had almost felt more alone now than whilst underground in Temple Tempus. He slugged himself up to the door of one of the more in-tact houses and went inside. The innards were extremely inviting, even for a partially collapsed building. It was decorated with torn and dust covered, however rather luxurious furnishings. Derik walked over to a small table in the middle of the room and noticed a fairly in-tact piece of parchment lying on the floor beside the table. He bent down picking it up immediately noticing a typical handwritten letter format and read it aloud.

"*Mother and Father,*

I am doing as you suggested and am going to 'The Sanctuary of the Ancients' to hide. I overheard Mrs Renkins from next-door telling Mr Sarrin that the army is drawing nearer and it won't be long until war is upon us. Mother, I'm scared! I hope you and Father return home soon. I love you both dearly.

Elissa xo"

Derik put the parchment on the table and looked toward a frame unevenly hanging on the wall between two large gilded candlestick holders. The family in the picture appeared to be quite peaceful which slipped Derik's thoughts to the family he never got to know, but was interrupted by an eerie giggle coming from outside. He began to wonder if he was delirious from not being in contact with people for months and as he neared the doorway he was caught by surprise when a blur flew by the house. He ran outside and suddenly stopped short struggling to make sense of what he had just seen; this was after all the first time he had ever seen somebody run right through a tree before.

"Ok, now I know I've gone mad," he said to himself as he tried to shake his head clean of delirium. Derik walked over to the tree running his fingers across lettering he noticed etched into the bark;

'Elissa .W. loves Junie .M'

Another giggle echoed through the empty village sending a jolt of terror through to Derik's bones. He turned south and began to run as fast as his legs would carry him when he noticed a bright blur running just ahead, veering sharply off to the left. By the time Derik had reached the path the blur had disappeared, his thoughts were beginning to become more rational and slowing to a normal walking pace, he decided to follow what he was now absolutely sure was simply somebody toying with him.

Leading Derik playfully to the outskirts of the other side of the village the distant blur vanished underneath the low-lying branches of a large tree as the path opened into a vast clearing, where a grand stone temple stood like an untouchable pillar of the Gods. Derik approached the slightly ajar doors. He slowly and silently ambled his way through the hallways of the temple to an impressive chapel room. Seats lined either side, a wide walkway running the centre, but everything seemed to be driving a focus toward a statue of a fierce looking blue Mystic at the base, a golden jewel crowned between its eyes.

The jewel was mesmerising and the pull was too much for Derik as he found his feet had carried him to the base of the statue. He reached his hand up and let his fingers brush the scaly stone head and as his hand slipped over the jewel, it drove deep into the Mystic's skull.

The sound of stone scraping across stone filled the temple but Derik could not see any movement from the walls, floor or roof. He slipped his hand down the statue and stepped to the side, his fingertips running along the stone statue base.

As he stepped over a piece of fallen roof covering the floor, a slight breeze blew across his leg. Derik bent down to inspect the piece of stone roof and mustering up what energy he had left, he pushed hard on the stone and shifted it from the place it had been laying to reveal a small opening in the floor; a hidden cavity.

An eerily warm breeze blew softly out of the opening and carried past Derik's skin running chills down his spine.

Although hesitant to enter the uninviting staircase leading into darkness, Derik hoped he might find some preserved rations to fill a supply that was now down to the last Marland bread crumb. Taking a deep breath, he walked steadily down the spiralling staircase.

The air at the bottom had a slight tang to the taste but Derik could not make out much of the dark room. The only available light sneaking through a crack on a wall, reflecting from a small mirror and ending in an illuminated circle on the floor. A small arrow engraved in the base of the mirror pointed at a wall on the opposite side of the room where Derik could just make out the frame of another reflective surface. He lifted the mirror in front of him toward the second and the underground cavity flooded with light.

As he looked around the room a dark heap hunched beside a small crate caught his eye. A skeletal figure of a young girl, surely no more than 10 to 12 years old and wearing the remains of a tattered dress, was the last thing Derik expected to find.

"What happened to this place?" Derik's deepened tone bounced from the floor as he crouched, looking into the deep dark and empty eye sockets. He followed the empty gaze toward the girl's skeletal hands, where the pages of a small notebook poked out from the sunken fingers.

Derik reached out and as he brushed the cover of the notebook, the hands of the girl fractured and fell to the floor, the rest of her body following. Derik winced. He glared at the notebook in his hands, the name 'ELISSA' stitched into the cover in golden letters.

"I guess your name was Elissa," Derik whispered opening the cover.

'This diary belongs to Elissa Wilkinson. For her eyes only!'

'Well, I've already read the first page and clearly you aren't going to mind,' Derik thought, nodding to Elissa compassionately as he turned to the next page and began to read Elissa's diary.

29th Ventus

Dear Diary,

This is the first of many long days I might spend hidden in the temple. Mrs Renkins says that the army is only a day away, so I have taken refuge down here until they pass through. Then I hope to find my parents. I'm frightened.

Elissa .W

30th Ventus

Dear Diary,

I can hear people scuttling above me, but I do not yet hear sounds of battle. I wish that Junie did not have to fight. I do hope he will be all right. I just wish that this would all end. Queen Elanore will save us, I just know it.

Elissa .W

31st Ventus

Dear Diary,

It has begun. I hear the voices of the townspeople I know and love; their screams, cries for help. I wish there was something I could do. I have only two days of rations left. Mother, Father... Junie my heart and prayers are with you all.

Elissa .W

32nd Ventus

Dear Diary,

I have just seen the most horrible of sights. I snuck upstairs to steal a look at what was happening and as I peered out the trapdoor, I saw the one thing I never in my life wanted to see. He did it to protect me. He sacrificed himself to keep my location a secret, to save my life...Oh Junie! Why would you give your life for mine? My heart is empty. If I ever survive this, I will not rest until I find the Altāsian who took you from me!

Elissa .W

As Derik read the diary his face filled with horror.

"You poor girl! You saw the love of your life slain in front of you," Derik said as he looked into where her eyes should be, quickly looking back to the next page.

33rd Ventus

Dear Diary,

My rations have run out and the war still remains. I have but scraps left. I can hear the dying roar of the Mystics our Queen left to protect us. I wish this horrid nightmare would end. I miss my family dearly. If they die, then I would have no reason to live.

Elissa .W

34th Ventus

Dear Diary,

I'm trapped! Something is blocking the trapdoor. The fighting came to a halt just before midday and for hours I lay here listening to the eerie silence. I decided to see what was happening and I cannot get out. I am very hungry!

Elissa .W

"She was trapped! After all she had seen and been through; she was trapped down here to die, alone," Derik whispered, worry lines stretching across his now grief stricken forehead as he sympathised with the girl's struggle of being trapped.

1st Tenshri

Dear Diary,

I fear that this is the end. I can feel myself growing weak, drawing closer to my death. I have a message for my parents, if they ever find me. I LOVE YOU BOTH DEARLY!

Elissa .W

2nd Tenshri

Dear Diary,

It is becoming harder to write, to concentrate ... harder to stay awake. Where is our Queen?

Elissa .W

2nd Tenshri

Dear Diary,

It is becoming harder to write, to concentrate ... harder to stay awake. Where is our Queen?

Elissa .W

3rd Tenshri

Dear Diary,

The pain is all but gone. I feel nothing. I cannot go on like this. I have to get out. Help Me...somebody!

Elissa .W

4th Tenshri

Dear Diary,

No more! Death has become me...

Derik turned to the next page only to discover it was blank and overcome by the sadness of such a tragic end for this poor girl he stood up and bowed his head in a sign of respect.

"At least you'll remain a memory," Derik whispered to the motionless bones as he slid the timeworn diary into his pack

Not wanting to face the same end that Elissa did, Derik turned for the stairs and determination fuelled his stomping feet as he made his way back up to the temple.

Back in the open air, Derik clutched his starved stomach in agony as he dredged his way to the path and followed it back toward the village, turning south and hoping there would be another village, one with living beings, as he headed home toward Lūnam; the legend of Altāsia's past buzzing through his mind.

CHAPTER 6

MIRUS

Derik watched the piece of string he had pulled from the lining in the side of his pack and fashioned into a fishing line bob up and down in the murky water.

"Come on! Take the bait, I'm starving!" Derik's frustration grew as his stomach grumbled louder. An hour had passed since he had arrived at the small lake outside the town in ruins and all he had managed to catch was a very small mud fish, which was only useful as bait.

"This is ridiculous," he said as he pulled the line in again. Reaching the bank, a sudden jolt on the line hauled it from Derik's hands. Reacting as quickly as his tired aching bones would let him he threw out his hands in the hope of catching the line before it sunk. Losing his balance, he stumbled face first into the muddy marshes.

The waist deep water seeped into Derik's clothes and he quickly reached both hands in to heave himself up when his hand pushed against a smooth surface in the water. Reaching in to the murky waters he pulled up a large muscle that fit in the palm of his hand.

"Not as tasty as fish but you will have to do my little friend," Derik said throwing the mollusc onto the sandbank and reaching in, in search of another.

"Only a few more and that should make a good meal," he said to the next mollusc he removed and he once again reached down into the murky water. But as the water dribbled from what he had expected to be another mollusc, it was not a shell he was holding but half of a stone. He turned it over in his hands and could not believe his eyes. There was something very familiar about the stone's shape and markings etched into it. He was holding the other half of the strange Mystic Stone that Xardos had in Waterfall Valley. Derik examined the markings he had been longing to get a closer look at since first laying eyes on it at the Metaprep.

"The etching's power was said to be incredibly great according to the book in Waterfall Valley. So what was it used for?" Derik wondered aloud as he traced the markings with his finger.

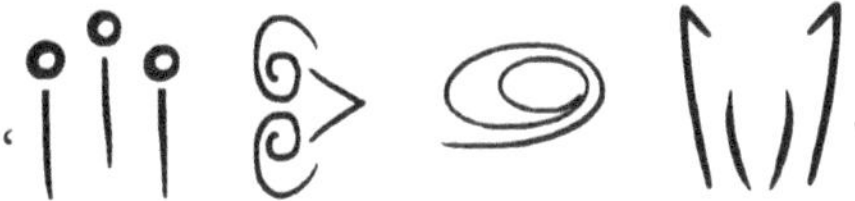

As night began to fall, the two moons of Tellūs rose from beyond the horizon and for the first time in weeks a brilliant night sky littered with streams of glowing specks was a sight that Derik had longed for. He sat by the banks of the Northern Marshes and took two small stones from the ground, striking them together. A group of sparks jumped into the pile of kindling he had gathered. Small flames began to lick the bark from the wood lighting the area with a warm glow.

He reached into his pack removing a piece of cloth and wrapped the half stone he had discovered earlier, returning it to his pocket for safekeeping and lay his head on his pack, the warming flames still flickering brightly.

The early morning moisture was icy against the beads of sweat dripping down Derik's face and the hammering heartbeat against the inside of his chest was pounding through his head. Derik often dreamed and this particular dream was one that had plagued him since arriving at Altāsia; the death of his mother. He lay on the bank of the Northern Marshes, his thoughts lingering in the fragments he remembered from the past of his infant self.

The fire was still burning and a great deal of warmth radiated from behind. He rolled over to warm his chest and stared into the embers, when the soft crunch of approaching footsteps made his ears prick. Derik held his breath straining against the silence as the light taps came closer, stopping just behind. He forcefully pushed against the ground, rolling back and knocked the assailant off their feet.

A shrill scream followed by a heavy thump left Derik face-to-face with a girl wearing a hooded black shawl. Crawling backwards Derik rapidly retreated from the low-lit girl sitting in front of him, questions thundering through his mind.

"Who are you?? A..a..and what do you want?" Derik called back to the strange looking girl from a safe distance, feeling he had spoken in a brute enough voice to make his assailant think he was not to be messed with.

"My name is Mirus," the girl shouted back in a soft almost mesmerising voice.

"Mirus!?" Derik whispered to himself. "What kind of a name is that?"

Derik got to his feet, his mind again flooding with questions. He slowly inched his way over to the girl still sitting on the ground and asked her for her name again, as he was sure he had heard wrong and again she answered with Mirus.

The girl reached out a hand and looked up at Derik while he tried to comprehend her name.

"Well Derik, are you going to help me up?" She asked with anticipation and excitement washing across her perfect face.

"How do you know my name? I've never met you before, have I?" Derik asked as he took hold of her hand helping Mirus to her feet.

"All will be explained in time," she whispered, staring hypnotically into Derik's eyes. "And well...it's not so much what I want with you, but what you have that I need!!"

"What could I have that you want?" Derik's forehead wrinkled as he awaited an answer.

"Please, Derik. I cannot explain here."

"What do you mean you can't explain *here*?"

"Follow me. My cabin is just a short walk from here and only there can I explain."

A thunderous laugh escaped Derik's lips. "What makes you think I'm going anywhere with someone that I don't know or trust?"

"Arrgh, Derik." Mirus looked over her shoulder, leaning in close to Derik's ear.

"Because I know what the stone is! And I know what happened in that city of ruins!" she whispered.

Confusion swept over Derik. Had she seen him discover the half stone in the marshes?

"What stone. I don't know what you are talking about?"

"Quiet...you never know who might be listening. I *will* tell you everything Derik, you *must* trust me," Mirus said, twirling around and running south into morning fog.

"Well, I am heading south anyway," Derik shrugged, not quite in earshot of Mirus anymore.

Catching his breath Derik entered the wooden doors of Mirus's cabin and walked over to the table she was already sitting patiently at and pulled out the chair across from her.

"Ok...first of all I would like to know how you knew that I had the stone. I had only just found it!" Derik explained.

"I know. Honestly, well I've kinda been following you since you left Lūnam," replied Mirus lifting her hand to an unlit candle and lighting it with the flick of her wrist.

"How did you do that?" Derik's attention was suddenly drawn away from the conversation.

"Let's keep to the topic shall we and all will be explained. Now where was I? Yes...that's right. I had been searching for you for a long time."

"What's so special about me?" Derik interrupted, wondering how long this girl had been searching for him, and why!

"The answer to that lays in a legend born more than one hundred and twenty years ago. My great grandfather Argonus was at a crisis point in his time."

Derik interrupted once again, "What can any of this have to do with your past?" he said still struggling to make sense of what she was saying.

"Listen! Now! The balance of purity and darkness was shifting across Altāsia and great grandpa Argonus was running out of time. The land was being overthrown by Elanore."

"Elanore! I have heard the tales of the terror she caused and I read about her in a diary I found in the destroyed city." Derik replied, happy he was finally starting to make sense of what Mirus was saying.

"Yes, Elanore was the cause of many problems for a lot of people. She was one of the most powerful enchanters of her time and had this idea that everyone was out to get her because of the Trials, so instead of using her powers for good, she let darkness flood her soul and that was when the stone you have the other half to was created."

Derik took the wrapped stone from his pocket and placed it on the table in front of him.

"First...what are the Trials?" he asked cocking his head to the side in confusion.

"The Storm Lake Trials...but we will get to that later."

Derik shrugged his shoulders. "Well, I saw the markings from this stone on the walls and pillars of a temple in the city of ruins." He and Mirus stared at the half stone in awe and fear. "Do you know what it says?" he followed.

"It is written in the language of the Ancients. These inscriptions were an ancient oracle, a means of communication between the knowledge of our subconscious and the material world. A means of gaining unimaginable power," Mirus replied, her eyes darting briefly from the stone to Derik's face. "The incantation inscribed on the full stone must never be uttered aloud but a rough translation will suffice:

"Who possess this stone can harness the strength of the shadow mana of the ancients to access and control the energy of the Mystics." Mirus's voice trailed off and the room was left in silence.

"So this stone was used for ... evil?" Derik asked.

"Yes. Elanore created this stone so that she could build an unstoppable army. The stone was used to control the mind of the Mystics. Every order that Elanore made, all Mystics under her power obeyed. She travelled Altāsia destroying villages, land and enslaving all who survived."

"That's what Elissa was talking about in her diary! But in her diary she referred to Elanore as her Queen." Derik interrupted.

"Some saw her as a goddess and joined her regime, but that didn't stop her from taking their lives."

Derik's face dropped as he realised the utter maliciousness that was Elanore. "Oh."

Mirus simply nodded and continued. "So! My great grandfather. He was the only person powerful enough to stop her reign of terror and after many, many months of planning he finally succeeded, but at a terrible cost. He cast an entrapment spell and ensnared Elanore within the stone splitting it in two and sending the pieces far from one another to ensure they would never be reunited."

"Whoa! And what happens when the two halves come together?" Derik asked.

"Elanore will again be unleashed and there will be no stopping her," explained Mirus.

Derik sat amazed at what he had just heard. Everything finally began to make sense as all the pieces of information combined in his mind to create the whole story.

"What was the cost?" Derik asked realising that Mirus hadn't finished.

"The cost was great to our land. We lost so many lives, but the curse was too much for the Mystics and after the hold on their minds was broken free, their life force faded from our land forever," Mirus replied.

Derik was surprised at what he had just heard. Mystics had to still exist, he was sure of that. "Wait, they can't be extinct! I was chased through the Forest of Night by a dirty great Mystic. It nearly got me killed."

Mirus' face suddenly dropped and clearing her throat she began her confession. "Uuumm, I may have had something to do with that. You see, I noticed you had entered the forest and there was something I wanted for you to find. So, I sort of pushed you in the right direction and conjured the shadow of a Mystic. But don't worry it was only an illusion to scare you into running to the cabin," Mirus quickly added seeing Derik's face drop. "Once you'd reached the cabin, I made the shadow vanish."

"But how did you conjure the ...you're a...a..." Derik trailed off. He couldn't believe the words that were coming from his mouth.

"An enchanter you mean? Yes, Derik I am!" Mirus replied, a smile sliding up the side of her face.

The word enchanter made the hairs on the back of Derik's neck stand to attention and he quickly changed the subject.

"At least I know I didn't just imagine it!" Derik whispered, a natural danger response beginning to run through every inch of his body, screaming for him to run from the enchanter. But his curiosity had proven to be stronger than fear in the past and these circumstances were no different so Derik continued. "There is another thing that I don't quite get. Why were you looking for *me* in the first place?"

"Well, when Argonus was alive his power rivalled that of Elanore which is why he undertook the task of stopping her. But just before his death he left me a piece of parchment that explained he would one day return when threat was to again plague Altāsia. When I heard of a boy with a glowing blue pendant falling from the sky in Lūnam I knew you had to be him...that blue stone used to belong to my great grandfather. He forged it himself!"

"So, you're telling me that I am your... that I am Argonus?"

Mirus went wide eyed and burst into an indulgent laughter. "Well not physically speaking of course but I believe his energy, his spirit, at least in part, is inside of you, which means that

Elanore's essence is regaining strength and Altāsia is once more under threat."

The air in the room fell still as the two sat surrounded only by the sound of the almost inaudible chatter of insects outside, basking in the cover of night.

"So now Derik, you understand why I saved you at the lake in the forest." Mirus interrupted the silence.

"That was you?!" Derik said as his thoughts drifted back to plunging into the icy cold water.

Mirus nodded her head and Derik sat astonished at what he had just been told; his head filling with questions faster than answers were clicking into place. Trying to decide where to begin asking, a loud grumbling rippled through his stomach interrupting the brief silence.

"Would you like something to eat?" Mirus asked as a clever looking smile reached across her face.

"Yes. Please!" Derik eagerly replied back as another rumble drifted from his stomach, his face burning with embarrassment.

Mirus lowered her head and begun chanting quietly, the table suddenly filling with a collection of delicious foods. It had been so long since Derik had had a decent meal and he began to shovel handfuls of food into his mouth.

"I don't know how you did that but thanks," Derik muffled through a mouthful of Marland bread.

"You're welcome," Mirus replied a sweet smile forming on her face as she also began eating the feast set out before them.

"That was delicious. I don't think I have ever eaten so much in my life," Derik said as he got up from the table and lay down on the bedding that Mirus had set out for him.

"When we wake, we will go into Lumen Village and fill up your rations," Mirus whispered as she put out the lamps and lay down in her own bed. The comfort reminded Derik of his bed that seemed so far away...home. He cuddled up to the soft blankets falling into a deep sleep.

The sun shining brightly in the clear blue sky was almost as nice as the beautiful song being whistled by the morning birds and a permanent smile seemed to be fixed on Derik's face. Being in the company of another person was very different from when he'd begun his journey. It was better he decided.

As they neared the hill ahead, sounds of a lively village drifted past Derik's ears and with a small excited half jump he quickened his pace. Passing Mirus to reach the top of the hill first, all of his senses suddenly becoming exposed to the magnificent sights, smells and sounds of a busy morning market below.

"Well, what do you need first?" Mirus began as she reached Derik's side.

Stunned a little Derik shook his head and tried to focus.

"Why don't you just, you know, use your *gift* to get the things I need?"

"Derik it doesn't just come from thin air you know. It's sort of like a transferral of energies. And besides nobody around here knows I can do the things I can and I'd like to keep it that way."

"Oh. Right. Sorry!" Derik nodded understandably considering he had grown up learning enchanters were not to be trusted and pointed at a building with 'Store' written in bold script on the window front.

"We should go there first, so I can stock up on food."

"Great. You head in and I will meet you back here in a minute, I have to pick something up from a friend," Mirus said as she politely pushed her way through the sea of people flooding the streets for the market.

Derik walked into the crowded doorway and began to squeeze through the small three aisle room collecting what items he could reach. He pushed his way through to the counter where a small flustered man stood frantically zipping from customer to customer and when it was his turn to be served the man simply snatched the coins from Derik's hand. Derik stood astonished for a moment and quickly picked up his items. The group surrounding Derik suddenly shuffled down to allow the next customer in and in the hullabaloo he was hustled out the doorway and back into the busy streets. Desperately his eyes searched for a safe, vacant spot to wait for Mirus and as the group in front of him moved on into the Market Square a park bench came into view across from the store, Derik rushing to sit before the spot was taken.

Five minutes had past when the deep blue, layered dress Mirus was wearing that day caught Derik's attention through the crowd of colours. As she pushed her way through, Derik noticed a long thin pole shaped package wrapped in parchment clutched tightly in her hands.

"What's that?" Derik called curiously as Mirus reached the seat he was on.

"I will show you when we get out of the village," Mirus replied, gesturing for him to follow her.

When they returned to the cabin Mirus quickly ran over to her bed and placed the package down.

"So, what is it?" Derik asked again now that they were out of range from prying eyes and ears.

"This is my great grandfather's old staff!" Mirus replied, unwrapping the parcel carefully, a look of great excitement gleaming in her eyes.

"What's with the enthusiasm?" Derik asked.

"This very staff was used to ensnare Elanore. It hasn't been used for over a century. After Argonus passed he asked for me to keep it safe. I decided it would be best kept safe in a neutral place. I hid it in the floorboards of the Lumen Village Library," Mirus stated holding up the crystal staff, the candlelight beaming through the green gem at the tip.

"This staff has contained the power that great grandpa Argonus once wielded. With the right teachings, you Derik can wield these powers."

"Powers? What kind of powers?" Derik asked, sceptical tones waving through his voice.

"The power to conjure, to [illegible] well anything your heart desires. If your soul is who I think it is you can do anything. I've seen great grandpa Argonus achieve amazing feats with this very staff."

"Exactly how long have you been alive, Mirus?" Derik asked, his attention suddenly drawn from the staff as he realised she had again made reference to seeming to know the last century as if she'd lived it.

"Alive...ha, how long? I guess you could just say I have seen many seasons!" The words escaped Mirus' lips as if she had rehearsed this very moment or lived it many times.

"Ok Derik, now it's my turn to get some answers! Why did you leave Lūnam?"

Derik sat for a moment wondering if he should share such a personal piece of himself with an almost complete stranger.

"Uuhh, well...I ah." The words escaped him for a moment as images of his mother flooded his mind.

"Well, since you've been following me you surely know I arrived at Lūnam during a storm that destroyed the ship I was on, right?!" Derik paused again for a moment trying to find the right words. "My mother lost her life that night and almost every night since I have had this dream, well it's more of a memory I think. She tells me about my great grandfather, 'The Adventurer,' and I guess in their memory I felt I needed to go on my own adventure."

Mirus stood stunned, a tear falling from her eye. She turned and tapped the tip of her boot onto the floor twirling it in anxiousness.

"Derik, I'm so sorry, I didn't mean to..." Derik cut Mirus off short. "Don't worry Mirus, it's ok, I've had a lot of time to get used to the idea of not having my family around, but I do miss Ranūl a lot, he's my adopted...carer, I guess. But I think of him more as my father."

"Does this mean you have decided to go home to Lūnam?" Mirus asked intriguingly.

For a moment, the idea of home seemed like the most comfortable place to be after all he had been through but after what Mirus had just discussed with him, Derik knew that he was now part of something much greater; a new legend of Altāsia.

"I think we now have more important things to worry about, which reminds me. I know where the other half of the stone is!"

Mirus' face suddenly dropped and the sounds mumbling from her lips slowly became decipherable words. "How. Where? We must destroy both halves."

"It was in Waterfall Valley when I was there. A man had it in a box at the inn I stayed at. He was going to the Valley of Mystics too."

"Then it's decided, we must go to the Valley of Mystics and find this man and the stone." An awkward silence bled through the air in the room as they both sat in thought.

"Oh, and...," Derik said hoping to interrupt the silence.

"Yes, what is it?" Mirus replied.

"I have something for you. These were in the cabin in the Forest of Night," Derik said as he handed the small glass bottles to Mirus.

"These were my great grandfather's. That cabin was where he hid while planning his retaliation to Elanore's conquest. He made the best potions," Mirus said as she popped the cork to one of the bottles.

"They really work well. I drank one that was labelled '*Salbūris*' when I almost died after falling into an underground temple," Derik was unsure if he had said it right but Mirus didn't take her eyes from the bottles and so he continued. "Almost immediately after drinking it I was fine, actually better than fine."

"So that's what happened to you! I lost you for a couple of months and was heading home to my cabin when I saw you at the Northern Marshes," Mirus explained as she snuffed out the candlelight leaving the cabin in total darkness.

"I'm glad you did Mirus, I was starving before you came along," Derik chuckled as he pulled up the covers, lying down for the night. "I fell into an underground cave system. Actually, it was more like a maze. I still can't believe I managed to find my way out. I reckon I almost tried nearly every door to every room."

"I'm glad you found your way out, or Altāsia would be in some real trouble," Mirus' voice came from the dark as she too lay down to sleep.

"Night Mirus," Derik replied closing his eyes.

"Goodnight Derik," Mirus said as Derik began falling into the one of the most comfortable sleeps he'd had since he lay on his favourite pillow in Lūnam.

CHAPTER 7
CITY OF RAIN

The clouds overhead were dark and with no place in sight to run for shelter, Derik and Mirus felt hopeful they would soon find somewhere to escape the torrential downpour as they reached the top of a grand hill. Derik stopped, in awe, as his eyes fell upon a valley below overlooking a grand lake with waters as dark as the stormy sky. Perched along the lakeside, a gloomy city lured them in, offering an opportunity to escape the cold. The duo's legs couldn't seem to move fast enough as they raced through the torrential rain, hastening toward the closest of the city's stone buildings. Relief washed through Derik as they reached the hardwood entrance.

A tattered sign displaying Nave's Tavern swung and knocked against the door as the two pushed eagerly, almost tumbling as they stumbled inside.

The tavern was warmed by the heat emanating from the roaring of flames, licking high over the logs resting inside a rather elegant looking fireplace along the wall to their right. Not a sound escaped from the few locals enjoying the cosy indoors as each slowly turned on their stools and stared at the drenched duo dripping in the doorway.

"I'm going to try and dry off," Mirus said hopelessly, ringing her hair and aimlessly brushing her saturated robe as she headed for the fireplace.

"And I will go and get us something to eat," Derik replied, giving his head a quick flick from side to side to shake the water from his soaked mane. A short smile flashed across his face with even the thought of a hearty, hot meal as he stepped up to the bar.

The large words scribbled on the wall behind the bar began to make Derik's mouth fill with saliva. He swallowed and enthusiastically called to the barman, "Excuse me. Can I please order two servings of Phoenix Stock Soup?"

"Sure, I will have it ready in just a minute for you fella," the rather stocky and hairy man replied, wiping his hands on the stained apron hanging from his neck as he turned and headed through a swinging doorway leading to the back.

Derik took a seat on the only open stool by the bar as he waited for the soup and swivelled around to face Mirus who was now standing by the fireplace with her robe hanging on the long package containing the staff.

"Not from around 'ere are ye!" The hoarse voice surprised Derik, who almost toppled from the stool as he swivelled to face a man hunched over the bar beside him.

"No. I'm from Lūnam. I'm heading to Valley of Mystics," Derik replied, gripping onto the bar-top with both hands to regain his balance.

"I know ye be not from 'round 'ere 'cause ye be wet."

"Of course I'm wet, it's raining outside. Actually, it's bucketing down!" Derik's condescending tone matched his raised eyebrows and the barely noticeable shake of his head as he gestured toward the tavern's doorway.

"True, it be rainin' but it always be rainin' 'ere in Castrene. Course that be why it be known as the City of Rain."

"What do you mean it always rains here?"

"We be livin' close to ye old Storm Lake, which be cursed by the spirit of Gandalin. Terrible tale it is that took the dear lady's life."

The thought of eternal rain was almost unbelievable but taking into consideration the events that had taken place over close to the past 12 months, not a lot seemed to shock Derik anymore.

"Name's Pertell. Me family has called Castrene home for many a century."

Derik grew curious about the cursed city and the 'terrible tale' Pertell spoke of. "Why is it such a terrible tale?"

"Gandalin was Castrene's leader for near on 30 years, before me was born. But a terrible thing in the Storm Lake Trails took the dear girl's life and the city be cursed with her spirit ever since," Pertell said, taking a sip from the mug that sat in front of him.

"What a terrible story," Derik replied, not quite knowing why these trials could lead to taking the life of one of its participants.

"Umm…excuse me Pertell, but what exactly are the Storm Lake Trials?"

"The tournament have been in play each year since Gandalin had first rule of the city. It be a way to determine the family next to be crowned as the king or queen of our fine people."

"You use a tournament to determine who rules the city?" Derik questioned, thinking it was a bit odd that the random outcome of some silly game would determine who was in charge each year.

"The trials is the best way. It be a measure of courage, spirit, skill and determination. All that makes a good ruler," Pertell replied, rather annoyed at Derik's ignorance.

"Well, I am sure the trials are interesting," Derik replied, sensing Pertell's irritation and turning his attention back toward Mirus before he found himself caught in a bar fight that he knew he could not possibly win.

"Your soup is ready!" Derik's thoughts were appreciatively interrupted by the return of the barman.

"Oh, thank you," Derik replied handing over two gold coins in return.

Derik took the two bowls of soup and looked over his shoulder to Pertell. "Good luck in your trials."

Pertell simply nodded in response. Derik could feel the eyes on him from the townspeople in the room as he ambled over to where Mirus had scored them both a chair in front of the fireplace.

"Thank-you Derik," Mirus said as she picked up the spoon and began to drink from the steaming bowl Derik had passed her.

"Mirus, do you find anything strange about this place?" Derik asked curiously.

"I haven't taken too much notice to be honest," Mirus said, dismissing Derik's comment as she raised a spoon to her mouth, a satisfying smile reaching across her face as the soup's contents slid comfortably down her throat.

"I just had a very interesting conversation with a man by the bar," Derik said, breaking the silence through his own mouthful of soup.

"Interesting you say. And what exactly is it that he told you that was so interesting," Mirus replied, placing the spoon in her bowl.

"He told me about these trials that the city's people play every year to see who will be crowned their new leader."

"Trials? ...ahh, yes the Storm Lake Trails. I was going to tell you about those when we first met. It had slipped my mind through all the trouble you have caused me over the past few months."

Derik screwed his face up in retaliation. "Well, it was you who decided to stalk me remember...to you know, help save Tellūs and all."

Mirus' face fell into a relaxed state and closing her eyes she replied, "You were already on your way to Valley of Mystics anyway Derik, and not for any old reason. This is your destiny."

Derik shook his head and changed the conversation back to the trials. "So, what do you know about the Storm Lake Trials?"

"They were a noble way for this city's people to determine who was best to rule their day-to-day life and Gandalin was very skilled and incredibly good at winning them. The people never did mind because she brought prosperity to the land. That was until Elanore entered."

"You mean Elanore used to live here?" Derik replied wide eyed, shocked to learn the evil he was about to face was once part of the population that now surrounded him.

"Yes Derik, Elanore once lived within these city boundaries. That was until she used her mana to kill Gandalin during the trials in an attempt to gain rulership of the city. It is told that she bewitched Gandalin's father to enter the games. Using a transpose spell she disguised him as one of the other contestants, whom she had taken the life of before the trials began so as not to arouse suspicion. During the last round, Elanore cast a spell to make Gandalin's caeli root sludge fail and forced her bewitched father to hold her underneath the water until she could no longer hold her breath. Elanore was discovered when Gandalin's father transformed back in front of the shocked crowd and she was cast out from the town, shunned for her heinous act. She went to live in a cave North of where I found you after Temple Tempus and that's where she conjured the Mystic's Stone. Nobody had seen or heard from Elanore for decades until the day her reign of terror began. People say she was seeking vengeance for being exiled and had gone crazy and bitter living alone in the cave for so long…and the rest is history," Mirus said, lowering her head.

"You're telling me this place…and the trials are why Elanore turned all psychotically super powerful cuckoo crazy? Because she was shunned by the people she grew up with!"

"No Derik. Elanore's quest to conquer those around her began much earlier than the trials. She just used the townspeople turning their back on her as an excuse. A reason to feel that destroying the lives of others was the right thing to do."

Derik sat for a moment, stirring his spoon in the last of his soup.

"So why is the lake cursed by Gandalin. Didn't you say she was a prosperous leader? Why would she bring this terrible curse on the people she loved?"

"As good as she was Derik, Gandalin had her own intentions for starting the trials. She knew each year before the trials would begin, who it was that might beat her. She would use her mana and peer into her crystals to see what the outcome would be. If the crystals told her she would not be successful, she would be sure to knock the predicted winner out within the first two rounds."

"If that was so true, why didn't she see her death coming?" Derik replied, a smug look falling across his face.

"From the stories I hear, Elanore had cast a spell to cloud Gandalin's crystals, so when she looked into it for future sight all she saw was a grey clouded mist. Gandalin was a sore looser as in her mind she was always the one best to rule the city, and she wasn't wrong. Under her leadership the town blossomed and the trials brought many people from across Altāsia who stayed and spent their coins at the town's eateries and accommodations to watch. Gandalin though became suspicious when she could not foresee the outcome of the trials and decided that she would cast a hex. If anything should happen to her during the trials, the city would be cursed with eternal rain for all of time, thus depleting the wealth that she had built throughout the years," Mirus said, picking up her spoon and sipping the last of her soup.

Derik sat in amazement that Elanore was involved in the downfall of so many people in the land before she had even created the Mystic Stone.

"Woah. That's intense. Poor Gandalin," Derik said staring down into his bowl.

"So do you think we should find somewhere to stay the night," said Mirus, suddenly looking up from her now empty bowl and looking to break the sombre mood.

"Are you sure, I mean wouldn't it be better if we just kept moving," Derik replied impatiently, hoping she would get the hint he didn't want to spend the night in a curse drenched city.

"What do you mean Derik? I thought you wanted to rest."

"I suppose I could do with a night in a nice warm bed," Derik replied sheepishly.

"Well, I guess we should find somewhere that has vacancies so we can set in for the night. Trust me. You're going to need rest if what I'm beginning to think turns out to be correct." A convincing tone riddled through Mirus' voice.

Derik was beginning to get used to the constant concealment of Mirus's inner thoughts. "But I thought we *needed* to keep going. You know, saving the world and everything."

"Derik, I may be an enchanter but I too need my rest." Mirus whispered, leaning a little closer to Derik to avoid listening ears.

"Alright." Derik reluctantly agreed as he placed his bowl on the table, tailing Mirus as she headed out through the tavern's doors.

Mirus lifted her robe over both of their heads as they desperately squinted through the blinding rain for any sign of a residence that would provide them with shelter for the night. "Now... Where to begin?"

"That place over there looks good," Derik said pointing to a double story house with a 'Rooms Available' sign posted on the lawn.

"At the moment Derik I think anywhere looks good, just as long as it's indoors." The sarcasm bounced off Mirus' tongue.

Mirus' robe wasn't doing a very good job at keeping the two dry as they raced over to the house. Derik scrambled for the handle and held the door for Mirus as she rushed past. Mirus shook her robe and folded it over her arm, covering the wrapped staff so as not to draw any unnecessary attention as she approached the woman standing behind a counter in the entrance room's centre.

Derik stood and watched as the woman nodded and smiled, but his attention suddenly sharpened when his eyes flicked across the nametag that the woman was wearing.

'*No way...that can't be.*' Derik thought as he approached the counter beside Mirus, realising that his first glance was right; the woman's name was Melene *Wilkinson!*

"Excuse me; I'm sorry to pry but you wouldn't happen to be any relation of Elissa Wilkinson, would you?" A nervous bump in Derik's voice made Mirus chuckle to herself. As Elissa's name left Derik's lips, a surge of shock seemed to fall upon the heavier set, red headed inn keeper as she slumped over the counter.

"Yes," Melene said hesitantly. "The cousin of my grandmother ...her name was Elissa. But she was lost in the war brought on by Elanore and was never found. How could you possibly know about her? She's been missing for over a century. Please! You must tell me what you know?" Melene began questioning Derik before falling silent. Her tired hazel eyes wide as she awaited his answers.

Derik felt he was stuck in a tight situation. He didn't want to upset this poor woman and he didn't quite know where to start.

"I found her diary in a small town to the North of this city," Derik said, sneaking around the subject of Elissa herself.

He reached into his pack, pulled out the diary and handed it to Melene who rapidly began flipping through the pages. As she reached the final entry, tears streamed down her cheeks, forming puddles as they dripped on to the counter. Derik couldn't tell whether they were tears of contentment or grief.

"Thank you. I am eternally grateful," Melene said through the small short breaths she was taking while flipping again through the sorrow bound pages.

Smiling awkwardly, Derik reached to his side to retrieve his pouch of coins to pay for their stay, and noticed it was no longer hanging on his belt.

Derik's cheeks flushed with red and he turned to Mirus, shooting her a confused look.

Mirus approached the counter, pulling Derik's arm to turn them away from Melene's prying ears.

"What is the matter Derik?" she said, matching the same confused look he had just given her.

"I can't find my coins to pay for the room. They were on a pouch hanging from my belt."

"Maybe the pouch fell off somewhere," Mirus said, trying to give Derik some hope, and trying to convince herself they would find it in order to spend the night in a comfortable room.

"Maybe they fell off while we were running through the rain," Derik said, turning to Melene and promising her they would be back in a moment.

The two returned to the drenched outdoors, desperately searching the ground between them and the tavern.

"I can't see it," Mirus said, wiping her face.

"How can we see anything through this?" Defeat quivering in Derik's voice.

"Maybe she will take mercy on us because I gave her the diary," Derik said, raising his eyebrows in search of hope on Mirus' face.

"I'm not sure that is going to happen Derik, but at this point we have no other option."

Derik and Mirus turned back to the door, a loud squelching echoed as they made their way, heads lowered, to the counter. Melene was still flipping through the pages over and again, as if searching for hidden answers as to why Elissa perished in the way she had.

"Hi. Ahh...Melene," Derik slipped his arm up and rubbed the back of his head. "Look, I seem to have misplaced the coins I need to pay for our stay, but I was hoping...seeing as though I gave you the diary and all...what I mean to ask is."

Melene looked up from the now tear drenched pages of the diary.

"I'm sorry Derik, I am trying to make a living here. There are many travellers who come through and seek refuge from the rain and they are paying customers. I don't mean to sound ungrateful for what you have done, but I don't know that I can help you," Melene said, a frown falling across her face.

"But isn't there anything else we can do. I could really use a night in a warm bed," Derik pleaded.

Melene peered at the two drenched travellers dripping water all over her entrance room floor, her disappointed expression changing. "Maybe there is something you could do for me."

A building concern wrapped around the inside of Derik's throat as he watched Melene's frown transform into a wicked smile. He reluctantly cleared his throat and managed to croak a reply. "Yes. Anything."

"Well. This year's Storm Lake Trials are beginning tomorrow morning and I do not have anyone in my family to enter. There is only me. What if you were to enter in my family's place? The two of you. If you agree, I will let you stay here the night and I will feed you well in preparation for the trials." Melene stood in waiting while Derik and Mirus shot each other a worrisome look.

"Mirus." Derik suddenly broke the silence from the trio and pulled Mirus aside. "Can we spare one day? I mean the trials do sound like fun and we can only do our best. I mean it's not like she's asking us to win or anything." Derik pleaded his case. "And besides...a nice warm bed, a warm bath...free food."

The sound of a nice warm bath sounded pleasing to Mirus and she nodded her head in agreement.

"Alright! Melene, you have yourself a deal," Derik said reaching over the counter to shake her hand.

Melene smiled, producing two small keys and handing one to each of them.

"I will be up to gather you early tomorrow morning. The trials start at dawn and you will need to be fed an energising meal to get through the day. You might just win for me," she said with a wink.

Derik turned and walked back to Mirus and the two made their way up the stairs to their rooms.

"Are you sure we want to do this Derik? What if something were to go wrong?"

"Mirus. We will be fine. What's the worst that could happen?" Derik replied, knowing quite well he had a powerful enchanter by his side to help if danger were to arise.

"So, what was that 'diary' thing about?" Mirus asked Derik as they reached the top of the stairs.

"Oh, it was nothing, just doing a favour for someone. I don't think we should mention anything about where we're going and who we are going to be trying to stop to Melene though."

Mirus nodded in agreement.

"Anyway, I'm in the room next to you if you need me," Derik said as he handed Mirus a silver polished key.

"Thanks. I guess I will see you before dawn then," she replied sliding the key into the lock and entering her room.

The first thing that drew Derik's attention when he pushed open the door was how luxurious this room was compared to his room in Waterfall Valley. A lavish rug lined the floor and a double bed with silk sheets was elegantly placed against the wall with intricate line-paintings hanging above. But the most important thing that comforted Derik was the security; a lock on the door.

He threw his pack on the bed, falling backwards with arms outstretched and plopped his head into the pillows. The cosy mattress beneath forced a yawn from deep within Derik, coupled with a full body stretch. His legs reached out sideways knocking his pack, a wristband with a red stone rolled out and onto the bed.

'*Oh yeah. I forgot to show Mirus,*' Derik thought to himself, quickly scooping the wristband he had come across in Temple Tempus into his hands and sliding it into his pocket. He grabbed his key and excitedly ran into the hallway, hoping Mirus could shed some light on what it was.

Derik knocked lightly on Mirus' door hoping that she hadn't already gone to bed.

"Coming." Mirus' entrancing voice flowed under the door and into the hallway. The door opened and a look of surprise fell across her face.

"Oh. Derik, I thought you'd gone to bed. What can I do for you?"

"I'm sorry to bother you, but I forgot to show you this," Derik said as he took the band from his pocket and held it in the palm of his opened hand.

Judging by the reaction that was now clearly visible on Mirus' face, Derik decided it would be better discussed in private, but before he could draw his next breath Mirus grabbed his arm and yanked him into her room, slamming the door as she whirled the two of them to the bed.

"Where ever did you get that from?" Mirus asked in a silent and entrancing voice.

"I found it in Temple Tempus when I fell into that underground cavern."

"I thought that it had perished long ago. Tempus was lost after the war and all who knew of its whereabouts are now dead." Mirus' voice swayed intricately, as if she were in a trance.

"Mirus! Are you going to tell me what this is?" Derik said sternly trying to snap her back to reality.

"I have to see if this is what I believe it may be."

Mirus suddenly snatched the band from Derik's hands and chanted a few words that began a spectacular light show from the stone within the bracelet and the blue stone that had been hanging from Derik's neck since he was a baby.

"I just cannot believe this. This is truly your destiny Derik," Mirus quivered with a slight gleam in her eyes.

"What are you talking about?" Derik replied, trying to understand what was so special about these stones.

"You...I...My great grandfather...Argonus. He left me a piece of parchment right before he passed and on this piece of parchment was a riddle." Mirus began to explain, tapping her wrist three times revealing a piece of rolled parchment in a puff of smoke in her hand.

Mirus unrolled the tattered parchment and began to read; *"One will be given to the royal time. Another you will find where the moon beams climb. The final piece that will unlock the past is in the shrine where empowerment was cast.* I never fully understood what he was talking about, until I found you in Lūnam Village and saw your necklace."

"Ok, you have to stop doing this Mirus. Spit it out," Derik grumbled, finally feeling he needed to be filled in on her secrets.

"Well, when Argonus was born his father stripped him of his powers until he was old enough to respect them and the location this took place was later turned into a shrine in the Regius Ranges. They are not too far from here."

"And you're saying that Argonus stripped his powers again before he died. And to…what?…unlock them you need all three stones in this shrine?"

"Precisely! You're a quick learner Derik. I think that we should leave for the shrine as soon as we complete the trials tomorrow."

"But what about the Valley of Mystics? Sorry to keep hounding about this, but…weren't we going there to *save the world!*"

"Well, you won't be able to do much saving of the world without unlocking your abilities first."

"My…abilities?" Derik said, falling silent in deep questioning thought and walked toward the door in a daze.

"I will see you in the morning. Night Derik," Mirus' voice flowed into his ears, but he couldn't hear them.

Locking his own door behind him, Derik turned out the bedside lamp and lay in the darkness, not quite sure on what to do with the story Mirus had just revealed to him.

'*Could it be possible?*' he thought as he drifted into a hazy sleep.

CHAPTER 8
STORM LAKE TRIALS

Derik's eyes reluctantly slid open to a constant knocking on the door to his room. He looked to the window and seeing that the light of the morning was still yet to shine through, he threw the covers over his head, but the knocks persisted.

The sound of a key sliding through the door's lock and the door swinging wide drew a grumble from deep within Derik's throat and he pulled the blankets down from his face in time to see Mirus and Melene charging in. They approached a weary eyed Derik and each grabbed hold of one of his feet, dragging him out of the comfortably warm bed and onto the cold floorboards.

"Derik! Come on. We don't have time for this. You need to get yourself into action and down for breakfast. Melene has a lot to fill us in on. We need to know how the trials work so we have the best chance of winning," Mirus said, crossing her arms impatiently.

"Ok, ok. I won't be a minute," he replied waving them away, dragging himself from the floor and making his way to the washroom.

The downstairs kitchen wafted a delightful smell that seemed to draw Derik to it. Pulling a chair out from the table he joined Mirus and Melene at breakfast, shovelling the Marland, Phoenix eggs and beast slice laid out before him into his mouth and washing it down with the glass of milk Melene had passed to him. A look of shock fell on Melene's face upon never having seen anybody eat this way before.

"Whoa. Derik, slow down. You'll give yourself a stomach ache and we don't want that, do we? You have a big day ahead of you. You both do," Melene said, her face turning from shocked to nurturing as she looked from Derik's full cheeks to Mirus, who was eating her meal with the grace she always seemed to possess.

"I'm glad to see you're awake and full of life," Mirus said, shooting Derik a condescending smile.

"Wouldn't miss such a great breakfast...oh and the trials... for anything," he replied with a mouthful of food, a goofy smile growing across his face.

"Good, because we have a lot to go over," Melene said, pouring herself a glass of milk. "Now, first thing's first. You both need to know how the trials work."

Derik and Mirus both lifted their heads from their plates, their eyes fixed on Melene's.

"There are three rounds. The first will be a challenge, but if you manage to pass through it as one of the victor families, the next two rounds will be the ultimate test to your skills." Melene paused to gauge the reactions of Mirus and Derik, who were looking to each other with a supportive grin. "This first round is all about endurance and it tests to see if you are the right family to carry out ruling the city for the whole year, without failing to continue doing the best for your people. It involves a race around the lake."

Derik smiled a winning grin. "Well, I'm pretty fast on my feet; I'll have this one in the bag. What about you Mirus?" He looked to Mirus, his grin still wide.

"Yes. A race should be no problem at all," Mirus replied, matching his grin.

Melene frowned, "It's not just a race that will be before you. There are tasks and dangers that you will need to face throughout the race. They change each task and what dangers are ahead of you each year so as nobody can just win on learning the best way around them. This means I cannot give you tips to help you defeat this task. It will be all on your shoulders."

The hope within Derik and Mirus began to fade.

"It will be ok. Anything they can throw at us we can beat together. Right Mirus?" Derik said, the smile on his face showing a little less confidently.

"Let's move on, shall we?" Melene said, interrupting their worried glances. "The second round is mainly about skill and showing you can acquire that which you seek. This was brought into the trials to show that the victors have the ability to lead with true precision and a vision which they will achieve. You will be sent up in a bubble basket that will take you high above the lake where you will try to catch the glowing orbs. The more orbs that are caught by all challengers in this round will mean you will get more points to use in the final round. The orbs will be in movement, so mastering the direction of the bubble basket will be at your advantage. Others have had years to master this so you will more than likely be at a disadvantage here, but you have the vision to succeed. I already see that in you. Both of you." Melene said, trying to boost the duo's morale. "You will need to be cautious though. If you do not keep your eye on things, this could end in tragedy. I have seen many perish in this round only because they did not pay enough attention to ensure that other players did not collide with them. Falling from such a height never ends well."

Derik cleared the build-up of concern growing in his throat. "And what about the third round?" he asked cautiously, figuring if it gets more difficult as each round progresses, the final round will surely be one to steer them away from entering altogether.

"The third and final is the round which was the end for Gandalin. You must go below the lake's waters. Using the orbs that have been collected from the second round, you will need to gather as many as you can. They will be scattered across the underwaters. The dangers here are not for the weak of heart. You will not only be faced with the deep darkness of the waters, and the possibility of other challengers accidentally shooting you with a spear, but there are things...creatures that lurk beneath which you will need to be wary of. But if you collect more orbs than any other challenger, and you take at least two out of the three challenges, you will be crowned victors of my family and I will help lead this village back to prosperity. Ultimately, with all things standing in your way, you will never win unless you try," Melene said, smiling widely.

Derik looked to Melene and whispered his thoughts to Mirus. "Is she crazy?"

Mirus giggled an uncertain laugh and the two swallowed loudly.

"Alright Melene, we're as ready as we are ever going to be. We'll go upstairs to get prepared and be down in a moment," Mirus said, a sweet convincing smile leaving Melene feeling as though her team may just win.

"Do you really think we have any chance of winning?" A concerned quiver shook through Derik's voice as he and Mirus reached the top of the stairs.

"I think we have just as good a chance as anyone else does," Mirus replied calmly, shooting Derik a reassuring smile. "And besides, it sounds like it'll be fun."

"Yeah, fun but potentially life ending," Mirus' reassuring words slowly faded again from Derik's mind as it filled with thoughts of peril.

"I will make sure nothing happens to us Derik," Mirus replied as the two reached their rooms.

"I'll see you back here in a couple of minutes and remember Derik, the first round requires us to be fast, so wear something light."

"Something light? You do remember that it is pouring out there Mirus, maybe something warm would be better," Derik said, holding his arms around his torso and forcefully shivering to push his point.

"Stop being ridiculous Derik," Mirus said, reaching over and pulling Derik's arms back down to his side. "It won't matter what we are dressed in, we are still going to be drenched by the trial's end."

Derik turned to his door and looked back over his shoulder to Mirus. "I guess you're right. See you in a minute," he said, closing the door behind him.

Melene approached her two challengers standing at the front door and opened a large umbrella for the three of them, before stepping into the rain drenched outdoors.

"I have something for you both," Melene said as they neared the lake. She reached into her pocket and passed Derik and Mirus each a red armband, a phoenix draped around a shield embossed in gold on one side.

"What are these?" Mirus asked, taking hers and placing it around her wrist.

"Each family is asked to wear these during the trials. It helps to differentiate between the families."

"What's with the phoenix and shield?" Derik asked, pulling his armband above his elbow and rubbing his finger across the stitching.

"It's my family's crest. It's a little ironic considering the phoenix always reminds me of warmth and our family ended up in the one place in all of Altāsia that would be the least likely place to see one." Melene replied smiling proudly.

As the trio neared the lake's edge the buzz of excitement from the townspeople crowding around the lake could be felt in the saturated air, as their cheers echoed through the town.

"Welcome challenger families and spectators to the Storm Lake Trials. This year we are celebrating one fifty years and because of this the tasks are going to be more challenging than ever before. We have been lead pleasantly by the Elsar family for the past year after their grand and seemingly simple defeat of the trials last year," the voice of the games' administrator resonated though the pelting rain as the town turned to see Grimlan Elsar, last year's victor, emerge from behind the wooden stage set to the North of the lakes.

"Mirus. That's the drunken fool who spoke to me in the tavern about this town being cursed with eternal rain." Derik said, a smile forming on his face. "Surely we will have no problem beating him. I doubt he could even run from the starting line to the first tree."

Mirus turned to Derik, her condescending look matching her tone. "Sometimes things aren't always as they seem Derik."

The booming voice of the administrator interrupted their conversation.

"This year, the Elsar family will see a new entrant in the trials. The youngest of the Elsar family, Jeralin." The administrator and Grimlan both turned as a young, toned Jeralin took to the stage, his dark chin length, rain drenched dark hair dripping by his chiselled face.

Jeralin pumped his fists high into the air, his arms lowering to show his strength, his forearm muscles glistening through the rain.

"I don't know how well we are going to go against him though," Derik said, his shoulders slumping in defeat.

"We have just as good a chance as he does Derik, remember he doesn't know what the trials have in store any more than we do," Mirus stated, taking Derik's arm and leading them toward the challenger's arena.

An assembly of families gathered underneath the sheltered waiting area that towered above the first round's starting line, parents whispering words of hope and strength to their family's toughest competitors who would be taking part in the trials.

"This is it. This is where I leave you and pray to the Gods you will stay safe and help bring honour to my family," Melene said, wrapping her arms around both Derik and Mirus, hugging them tightly. "Now, you will need to decide who of you will enter. Only one challenger from each family can take on the trials."

Derik's left eye twitched with concern and stress. "You're only telling us this now Melene?" he stated, looking to Mirus for something that would reassure him that he would be safe if it were he who entered.

"I am sorry Derik, but the rules are the rules. Only one of you may enter officially. However, should the one you choose not succeed, each family is allowed one replacement."

"What do you mean 'not succeed'?" Mirus said turning to face Melene. "Surely you don't mean..."

"I'm afraid I do Mirus. Should one of you perish in any round, the other is deemed to take their place for the remainder of the trials."

Derik's face wrinkled with concern and he took a deep breath. "I will take the starting point. These trials can't be that hard, can they? I mean I managed to defeat an Ampharo in Temple Tempus. Surely I can conquer these trials." Derik said to Mirus, his lifted spirits showing on the outside, but shrivelling in his mind.

Mirus pulled Derik to the side, out of earshot of Melene. "Are you sure Derik? I am far more capable of staying alive than you are at this point and you are our only hope in defeating Elanore. I guess, all I'm saying is...this island and Tellūs needs you...I need you." Mirus whispered, her eyes looking deeply into Derik's.

Derik stood for a moment in frozen stasis. "No Mirus. I can win these trials. The first round is just a little race right? Even if I don't win, what's the worst that can happen?"

Mirus turned to Melene. "Derik will enter. We will do the best we can for your family," Mirus said with a reassuring smile, hoping Derik's confidence would get him through the first round.

"Challengers, take your place at the starting line." The administrator shouted, leading each family into a string of embraces. Mirus turned to Derik and stepped forward, wrapping her arms around him. "Good luck, Derik," she whispered into his ear before stepping back and following Melene to one of the sheltered grandstands.

Derik took a deep breath and swallowed loudly, which was apparently heard by Jeralin, who had taken his place right next to Derik at the starting line.

"Ha. Nervous are we?" Jeralin stated smugly.

"I'm not nervous at all, just eager to start," Derik replied, brushing the raindrops building on his face.

"Are you ready?" The administrator screeched, looking at each of the challengers along the starting line. "Let the Storm Lake Trials...begin!"

The moment the administrator's words faded, a deep horn blow sounded to signal the beginning of the trials, challengers racing eagerly ahead, leaving Derik and Jeralin at the starting line.

"What. Too scared to move?" Jeralin said, shooting Derik a superior grin.

"I was just trying to give the others a fighting chance," Derik replied as he raced ahead, turning to smile patronisingly back at Jeralin, who had begun to walk briskly and was looking to the tree line ahead with caution.

Derik jumped the first of seven hurdles that lay on the track before him, managing to pass two others who seemed to be struggling with the task.

"Huh. Maybe I might just have a chance here," he whispered to himself as he leaped over the second.

With his feet carrying him quickly over the last of the hurdles and making his way to the tree line, Derik turned back toward the starting line and noticed Jeralin was only but one hurdle behind him.

The trees ahead lined the lake, but were sparse enough that Derik decided they wouldn't make a dent in the speed he was gaining, until he saw a great log swing from the tree tops, rushing toward the ground at a breathtaking pace. Derik didn't have time to stop, the log brushing his arm with enough force to knock him to the muddy ground beneath.

"What on Tellūs was that?" Derik's question was interrupted by the squelching quicksteps of Jeralin as he sped past. "Having trouble already huh?" Jeralin smirked, carrying out a left hand spin as he dodged the next log that came whirling from the trees.

"Flumbar...I'll never catch him now," Derik grumbled, getting to his feet, shaking the mud from his arms.

From the sidelines, Mirus and Melene were recovering from a wince as they realised the log hadn't killed Derik and inched open their squinted eyes while they watched as Derik managed to dodge the next three swinging logs.

Melene turned to Mirus wide eyed, "Wow...and that was only the first hurdle," she said, doubt clearly already showing through her tone.

"Have a little faith Melene...he's just off to a rocky start. He'll shake it off," Mirus replied, turning back to watch eagerly, a slightly worried voice in her mind adding to her reply to Melene, '*I hope.*'

'*Ok, this isn't so bad,*' Derik thought to himself as he rounded the track to the north east of the lake, his growing confidence short lived as he saw what lay ahead. Two challengers were reaching desperately to pull themselves up from a thin wooden plank that created a bridge across the river that fed the lake to the east, their expressions filled with fear. As Derik approached, he soon realised their fear, seeing the scaly back of a large creature circling in the waters below.

Derik took a deep breath and called out to the two. "Don't worry, I'm coming. Hold on," but his words fell short as the two let go of the last of the grip they could muster, splashing into the river, both scrambling for the shore.

One wearing a blue armband made it to the shoreline and quickly pulled himself out of the water, running to a safe distance before turning back to make sure the creature hadn't followed. The other, wearing a green armband, had been caught up in the fast flowing river and pushed into the lake, the creature following close behind, its head rearing out of the water displaying a mouthful of double-rowed, spear headed teeth. The creature dipped underneath the dark waters and Derik watched on in horror as the challenger was dragged beneath the water's surface. He turned his head closing his eyes as a deep red swirl began to saturate the water around where the challenger had been.

The crowd breathed in sharply as a deep shock spread over them, some continuing to chatter gloomily amongst themselves as the gut-wrenching wails of the challenger's family flooded the arena.

"This is nuts," Derik whispered to himself. "What a tragic waste of a life." He turned his attention back to the thin plank and tried to focus, after all he didn't want to be the next meal for that creature. He took a wobbly step onto the plank, steadied himself and then followed with his other foot. He shuffled along slowly, inching forward before making it safely to the other side.

'*I take it back,*' Derik thought to himself while wiping his forehead with his arm. '*This IS bad!*'

"Two challengers down and tragically one of them lost to the jaws of the Crūnus," the administrator's voice echoed around the lakeside. "Halfway there and Jeralin takes the lead."

The words echoed through Derik's ears. "I can't let *HIM* win," he said, picking up the pace, blindly pushing ahead without knowing what perilous task may lay before him. As he rounded the next corner a large, shadowy wall appeared in the distance and as he neared it, it was clear it was no ordinary wall. Steel spikes were pushing in and out of the wooden structure from the ground to the top at a seemingly irregular pace. Two of the other challengers, one wearing a purple armband and one wearing teal, were standing at the bottom. Derik noticed they both seemed unsure of how to overcome such a life threatening task.

"Hey. Are you going to give it a go?" Derik asked the challenger with the purple armband.

"I don't wish to end up like the guy back there," he replied.

"Yeah. And I really don't want to die either," followed the girl wearing the teal armband.

The constant and irregular sound of scraping metal plunging out of the wood saw Derik share their views. "But how did Jeralin get over it?" Derik asked curiously.

"It was amazing. Not really sure how he did it and survived," the girl in the teal armband said.

"He just sort of dashed his way up. I think he might have been nicked a couple of times. It was a close call. Guess he really wants to win," the boy in the purple armband added.

Derik stood for a moment, watching and listening to the sounds of the spikes extending and retracting and closed his eyes in defeat. '*I can't do this. They're right, this will surely kill me if I try it.*' His thought was broken by the sudden realisation that there seemed to be a pattern to the sound of the spike wall. He opened his eyes and sure enough, while it was discreet, what he had heard was right. There was a pattern. He readied himself and as the last of the spikes at the bottom began to retract he leaped at the wall, the other two contenders gasping in disbelief.

At the top left, the blades shot from their holes, followed by the ones beneath them and both began to retract. Derik swiftly jumped to the left just as the ones below them extended, allowing for Derik to balance briefly before leaping for the top of the wall. As he scrambled over the ledge, the spikes had begun the round again at the top, narrowly missing his foot. The two challengers at the bottom were left stunned as Derik shot them a cheerful grin, raising his hand in salute before turning and jumping down the back of the wall.

CHAPTER 9
THE IGNIS CHARM

Once safely on the other side of the spike wall, Derik turned his attention back to his only remaining opponent for round one, Jeralin. He knew how much of a lead he had, but what was not clear was how many more obstacles were between him and the finish line, and more importantly how dangerous they were.

He took up pace once again rounding the lake to the west, the last leg. His eyes focussed on what seemed to be the finish line, but it was too far away to tell, and there didn't seem to be any obstacles in-between.

"I don't see Jeralin anywhere. I bet he's already passed the finish line," Derik said aloud, clenching his fists at the thought of losing to such an obnoxious person.

Taking the next few strides, Derik felt the ground beneath him shift and he fell into a muddy pit. Trap doors above him began to slowly close and his heart raced at the thought of being stuck in the pit with little to no oxygen. He began clawing at the slippery walls trying to find the top ledge but it was just beyond his reach. The doors above closed and all light was swallowed by darkness.

Derik wondered if the townspeople would just leave him there or if somebody would come to his rescue after the trials had finished, that is if he survived until then. '*Surely Mirus will get me out,*' he thought as he squinted, trying to adjust his eyesight to the endless black surrounding him.

Fumbling around in the dark, Derik's hands were slipping deep into the muddy floor and walls. His eyes still hadn't adjusted to the light when his hand slipped over something solid buried deep within the wall facing the finish line. He reached both hands in further and his fingers clenched around a pipe. He pulled, trying to release it from the wall, in hope he could use it to pry the doors open and find a way to climb out. It shifted slightly so he pulled again, his determination leading to triumph as he felt it shift. The more he pulled the more it edged closer to him. It seemed near enough that one more, hard yank should pull it free from the wall and so once more he pulled and a small amount of light flooded the pit.

Derik was left peering through a small doorway into a tight tunnel, with just enough light for him to make out his way forward. He got down on his hands and knees and began to crawl through the space, moving as fast as he could.

The further he went, the more light seemed to be flooding into the tunnel.

He reached an opening to the right that lead steeply to the surface.

Once outside, Derik turned on his heel and saw the finish line only a meter away. His feet pounded the muddy banks around the lake and he fell to his knees as he crossed the finish line.

"Congratulations challenger. You have crossed the line in second place." The booming voice of the administrator felt like a swift kick to his stomach as Derik realised that he had been outdone by Jeralin.

"Awe...flumbar," Derik said, pulling his boot off and watching a clump of mud plop to the ground.

"Derik! You did it." Came the beaming voice of Mirus. "I mean you didn't win, but you didn't die." Her sly, almost condescending voice only adding to Derik's frustration.

"Thanks, Mirus," he replied, rolling his eyes. "I bet you wouldn't have even made it half way through that race."

"Either way, we still have two rounds to go and so long as you win them both Derik, the city will be lead peacefully and strongly in my family's name," Melene intervened the almost childish spat between Derik and Mirus.

Derik turned and noticed that the bubble baskets had already been set in place for the second round, and a short tubby man was kneeling beside a large box, reaching in, pulling out an orb and winding it up with a key. The orb began to glow and floated into the sky above the lake, joining several others that were already in place.

"So, I'm guessing the others forfeited the round?" Derik asked.

"Yes. They were too weak. Actually, I am quite surprised you even made it." Jeralin's tone sent waves of irritation through Derik's body.

"Challengers, ready yourselves for the second round. Due to the unfortunate incident in the first round, the fallen challenger from the Riels family will be replaced for the remainder of the games," the administrator announced. "Please take up your position within your designated bubble basket."

"Good luck with this one Derik," Melene said, locking her fingers together and lifting her hands in hope. "Remember, watch out for the other challengers and the orbs."

Derik gave her a sharp nod and sneered at Jeralin as they both walked to their baskets. Climbing in, Derik awaited the starting horn.

The sound reverberated around the lakeside as each challenger let the rope loose holding their baskets in place. Derik grabbed hold of the steering handles and pushed on the inflator hanging down by the bubble sending him skyward. '*Gee, I don't even know how to fly this thing,*' he thought as he turned the handle toward the direction of the closest orb.

From the stands, Melene and Mirus instantly saw that Derik was on a collision course with another two challengers who had also decided the closest orb was their first target. Mirus cupped her hands to her mouth and raised her voice in an attempt to warn him, "Derik! Watch out for the others!" It fell on deaf ears as the resounding cheers egging the challengers on from the crowd drowned her out.

"What are we going to do?" Mirus asked Melene in panic.

"We can only hope that he notices in time," Melene replied turning back to the action of the trials and watching Derik intently.

The rain created a problem Derik hadn't anticipated and as he rose higher, the wind made it more difficult to steer. He began to drift off course, floating away from the orb. Clutching the handle tightly Derik pulled hard back toward the orb, but he had missed his chance. Two other contenders had already reached either side of the stationary orb and were attempting to reach it with scoops. But, to Derik's amazement, the orb darted away, knocking into another nearby and setting off a chain reaction that sent all of the orbs buzzing through the air around the lake.

"How the heck are we supposed to catch these?" Derik wondered, as he turned the handles sharply to the right, now more aware of the other challengers around him.

Derik picked up the scoop that was strung to the inside of his basket and decided the best way for him to succeed in this round was to watch carefully and track the paths of the orbs before intercepting. He turned his attention to one that was whizzing toward him and remembered Melene's warning about the orbs colliding with the bubble sending the baskets falling to the lake below. "Well here goes," he muttered cautiously to himself. He pushed the steering handle forward, gaining speed and reached the scoop out in front, the orb inching closer and closer.

"You snooze you lose!" Came the unfortunately familiar voice of Jeralin as he whirled in from the left, scooping up the orb, leaving Derik hanging with his arm out the side of the basket holding an empty scoop. "I really don't like you," Derik said aloud, knowing full well Jeralin was nowhere near earshot.

Derik decided to try his tactic again and turned his attention to another orb that was moving from his left toward the East end of the lake. "Gotcha!" Derik breathed a small sigh of relief as he netted his first orb.

His second wasn't as easy to capture and he spent what seemed like an eternity hunting it down and getting into the right position to scoop it up. "Two down," he said through a triumphant smile. His smile was short lived, as a loud boom from behind him triggered an instant reflex to cover his ears and he turned to see two bubble baskets had collided and were rapidly falling into the waters below. Two challengers broke through the water's surface and began frantically swimming to the lake's shore; both made it.

Derik whirled his head from left to right in search of his other three opponents realising they were each at opposite ends of the lake and each with two orbs glowing brightly through the nets in their baskets. '*I am still in with a chance. I just need to get a few more orbs,*' he thought as his eyes darted rapidly counting the remaining seven orbs whirling around the lake. "You're next," he said pushing his handle forward with full force.

"Yes! That's his third orb," Mirus said as she performed a little jump in her seat and clapped her hands together.

"He does seem to be doing quite well at this round," Melene replied. "But Jeralin also just captured his third," she continued.

"Come on Derik, I know you can do this." It was as though Mirus' encouraging words had reached Derik's ears as he netted his fourth orb, leaving four remaining.

Jeralin once again rushed past Derik chasing a rather fast moving orb. Derik ignored him and turned his attention to another orb at the far side of the lake. "You will be my next victim," Derik said through a smirk that lasted only a few moments as he saw the Riels family challenger swoop in and scoop it up. He too had four orbs in his basket. Derik searched the skies around the lake and noticed the other challenger had only three orbs and to his dismay he realised Jeralin also had four. It was still anybody's game. Not wanting to waste any more time he eyed his next target and shot to his right, scooping it up as it zipped past. Grabbing hold of his steering handle, Derik made a sharp left turn and was face on with Jeralin who was leaning over and scooping up another orb, leaving just one orb darting around the lake, seemingly attempting to evade capture.

"Don't worry yourself with this one, I've got it," Jeralin shouted, grasping his handles tightly and speeding off tailing the final orb.

"Not if I can help it," Derik replied, taking hold of his handles and speeding after Jeralin. As Derik neared Jeralin's basket the gap between the two bubbles narrowed. In his haste, Derik pulled on the inflator sending him flying directly above Jerlin's. As they neared the final orb, Derik gripped hold of his scoop and leaned over the basket. His balance wasn't on his side and he slipped over the edge, catching his feet on the top border of the basket. Dangling upside down, Derik had to keep his goal in mind, and again reached his scoop down, just in front of Jeralin's, swiping the final orb.

"I did it!" He cheered, before realising he was still stuck upside down hanging from a bubble basket that had nobody at the controls.

"Looks like you're in a spot of bother there. Why don't you hand over the orb and I'll net it in my basket and then lend you a hand." Jeralin's look matched his pompous tone.

"You wish," Derik replied, gripping the scoop's net with his left hand to keep the orb safe and reaching his other arm up, grappling for the basket. His hand clenched into the basket's side and with all he could muster he pulled, flicking his body upward. He grabbed hold of the edge of the basket as his feet unhooked leaving him hanging by one arm. Derik threw his other arm up, swinging the scoop and orb inside and grabbed hold of the basket's border, scrambling up and back to safety. He swiftly stood and took hold of the steering handle, sharply turning back toward the crowd, picking up the final orb and holding above his head in victory, turning to smile slyly at Jeralin before netting it.

The crowd erupted and Derik was met with Melene's two arms wrapping tightly around him as he exited his basket back on the shoreline.

"You were astounding out there Derik," she said hugging him tighter and rocking from side to side.

"Alright, I must admit you were pretty…," Mirus stopped short as she noticed Derik's look. "What?" She questioned.

"Am I right in saying you were just about to compliment me," Derik smirked.

"Well…ah…no…that is…I was simply going to say you finally managed to win a round," Mirus replied, looking away from Derik's fascinated stare.

"That's enough you two," Melene objected, stepping back and grabbing Derik by the shoulders. "The last round is by far the most perilous, and you need to be in the right headspace Derik."

"I've managed to stay alive so far," Derik replied shooting Melene a winning grin.

"That you have," she replied with an endearing chuckle. "Now we have to get you prepped. Each of the challengers is given a special herbal sludge that you need to coat the inside of your mouth with."

Derik screwed his face up sticking out his tongue. "What! Why?"

"It is an ancient recipe made from the root of a Caeli tree from the Forest of Light. The sludge absorbs the oxygen from the water, helping you breathe while collecting the orbs in the final round," Melene stated as a matter of fact.

"Ok," Derik reluctantly replied, as Melene swung him around on the spot by the shoulder and marched him towards the round three starting position.

The administrator's voice once again bellowed through the crowd. "Congratulations to the Wilkinson family for taking out round two. It was close but there can only be one winner. Which brings us to our final round. There were five orbs collected by the winning challenger for the Wilkinson family who successfully finished round two and those orbs have now been scattered below the lake's surface. Challengers, it is your job to procure as many as possible. Now get yourselves ready and remember to watch for the Crūnus that lurk beneath."

Derik picked up a small bowl containing a white sludge and scooped some onto his finger, reaching into his mouth and rubbing it along the inside of his cheeks. He paused for a moment and spat to the ground, rubbing his tongue on the back of his hand. "This stuff tastes awful," he said, while the other challengers looked on, giggling at his entertaining reaction. "Oh well, if it means I can breathe and beat Jeralin then…here goes." He reached back into the bowl and hesitantly continued rubbing the sludge along the inside of his mouth, coating it well.

He picked up a shooting spear and collection net from the pile left for the challengers and stood by the water's edge, the bulge in his throat moving to his chest as he took a deep breath.

The horn sounded for the final time and each of the challengers dove in hastily; Derik wondered if they had any fear of being eaten alive at all.

As Derik lifted his foot to follow suit, the boy from the Riels family broke the water's surface and quickly made his way back to the shoreline.

"Are you ok?" Derik's sympathy and concern was genuine and it must have come across that way as the Riels boy walked over to him and began to cry.

"I just can't bring myself to do it. My brother was just killed by one of those things, besides it's really not a fair game anymore. It's between you and Jeralin now," he said between sobs, slouching his shoulders and walking head down in shame back to his family in the stands. He was greeted with understanding and a tightly grasped hug from who Derik assumed was his mother.

"Well Jeralin. Here I come," Derik said, spinning back toward the lake and diving in.

The lake's waters were dark and the cold pierced down to Derik's flesh. '*The orbs. I need to find the orbs,*' he thought, swishing his head through the blackened waters in search of their emanating glow.

Derik reached his arms forward, pushing and kicking slowly through the water when he felt a throb in his chest. He had been holding his breath, his cheeks full of the last gasp of air he took before diving into the lake. Reluctantly, Derik opened his lips, allowing the water to flow into his mouth and instead of swallowing a gulp of water, he took a breath of air. The sludge had formed a barrier at the back of his throat, preventing the water from flowing down into his lungs, just as promised. '*Well, it's good to know I won't drown.*' He thought, reaching forward and propelling himself further into the depths of the lake.

The dark depths consumed Derik as he swam deeper. He could no longer see the flicker of dull light that indicated where the lake met the sky and he began to wonder whether he was swimming up, down, left or right.

'*I guess this will make it easier to spot one of the orbs.*' His thoughts were verified with the sudden appearance of a golden glow a few meters in front of him. Derik kicked ferociously toward the glowing light and smiled as he took hold of an orb, sloshing it into his carry net and he wondered how many orbs his opponent had already managed to snag.

Derik thought back to Jerlin's smirky grin and his brow wrinkled with determination as he pushed forward. '*I have to win this. Not only for Melene but so I can rub it in Jeralin's face.*' His thoughts once again interrupted by the sight of a soft glow in the near distance.

With two orbs now netted, Derik felt as though he had been swimming in circles having not detected any signs of light, another challenger or the Crūnus for what seemed like hours.

His concentration on the task at hand faded as the image of how wrinkly the skin on his hands would be once he finally finished the trials consumed his thoughts. He cringed at the sight in his mind but was soon reminded of where he was as his eyes caught a glimpse of another dim glow. Thrashing eagerly toward the orb, Derik froze, pushing against the water to hold his position as a shadow emerged from the depths. Its size didn't match the creature Derik had seen earlier in the trials but it simply could be a Crūnus' child.

Eyes wide and readying his spear to strike, Derik rolled his eyes as the shadow's features became apparent as Jeralin emerged from the deep. The two reached the orb simultaneously, each hurriedly reaching out their hands to grab what they thought was the winning orb. Derik reached his arm out to swish Jeralin's away and the two were locked in a battle to retrieve the orb, the water around them swirling ferociously.

With Jeralin and Derik's attention drawn to the orb, they had failed to realise the dark shadow emerging from beneath them, until the double-rowed teeth of the Crūnus snapped fiercely between them, pushing the orb into Derik's grasp. Derik swiftly snatched the orb, placing it into his net, swirling around as the Crūnus turned back toward the two challengers. Derik reached down, taking hold of his spear and without hesitation fired at the creature. The spear cut through the water, digging deep into the leg of the Crūnus. Derik could feel the rage of the creature as it swirled in agony before turning its attention to Derik, firing through the water at speed and jaws gaped as if ready to devour him. Over the shoulder of the Crūnus, Derik could make out the shadow of Jeralin, spear raised. Derik reached his hand out to signal Jeralin to stop, when the Crūnus squirmed once again as the spear penetrated through its body. The second strike further infuriated the Crūnus and it continued its propulsion through the lake's dark waters, striking Derik in the abdomen.

Derik's eyes opened slowly and as he regained his sight he found himself looking to the stormy skies above.

"Wh...what happened?" Derik's crackled voice whispering through the mutters of disbelief and astonishment of the crowd gathered around him.

"Shh. Derik. Try not to move." Mirus' voice was a welcoming sound.

Melene stepped forward and put a hand on Mirus' shoulder. "My dear, I do believe you have caused quite a disturbance with what you just did!" she said, gesturing for Mirus to look around at the townspeople.

"I saved his life is what I did Melene!" Mirus rebutted, her attention still focussed on the semi recovered, and rather drenched Derik.

"Yes...you did...but it was how you did it." Melene's awkward response mirrored the faces of the townspeople. "We haven't seen the likes of your kind here since Gandalin and Elanore." Melene continued, making reference to the incantation Mirus had cast, healing Derik's wound after being pulled from the water by Jeralin.

Derik sat up, clutching his abdomen, where he had felt the jagged jaws of the Crūnus embed deeply before losing consciousness within the lake.

"Once again...I owe you one Mirus," Derik said, the brilliant smile fading as he got to his feet and noticed the shock in the crowd. "What's wrong with them?" he asked, turning to Melene in confusion.

"Derik. We have not seen the power of the ancients used here since Elanore killed Gandalin. You can understand why some here are a little uneasy with that?" Melene queried.

"Oh. Yes. Of course. My apologies," Mirus said, turning to address the crowd. "Please. Accept my apologies. I come from a long line capable of performing acts of healing. I am far from the terror your ancestors had the unfortunate experience with and I can assure you my abilities do not go farther than that." Mirus said, darting a look at Derik that said '*Do not say a word.*'

Mirus' words seemed to be doing the job as the weight lifted from the air and the townspeople began to approach, some checking to ensure Derik was indeed ok and others cautiously thanking Mirus.

"Lucky you're still breathing." The condescending tone of Jeralin interrupted the obscure grin Derik was giving to those approaching him. "I mean if it wasn't for me, you would be Crūnus lunch," Jeralin continued.

Derik took a moment to gather his thoughts. "You rescued me from the waters?" Derik questioned, his face scrunched with confusion.

"You bet I did...I mean I didn't heal you or anything, but I got you out of the water after I took care of that nasty great Crūnus."

Derik took a step, holding a hand out to Jeralin. "Maybe you and I aren't that different after all Jeralin."

Jeralin leaned back and knocked Derik's hand out of the way. "Don't be so sure about that. I wouldn't have been stupid enough to put myself be in the path of the Crūnus in the first place." Jeralin's smug reply reminded Derik rather quickly of his urge to thump his fist into Jeralin's nose.

"Well. Thanks all the same," Derik replied, the two challenger's glaring exchanges broken by the booming sound of the administrator.

"We have our victor!" The voice reverberated around the lake as everyone began returning to their seat in the stands. "It was quite a close call there for a moment, however we didn't lose the Wilkinson family challenger. Also, it is apparent that he managed to net three orbs; one more than his closest challenger and two more than our challenger in last place. And so, it brings me great pleasure to announce that leadership shall be placed upon the WILKINSON FAMILY!"

As the administrator's words faded, Melene leaped to her feet and grabbed hold of Derik, pulling him so tightly to her body that he thought he was going to pass out again.

"Oh, thank you, thank you...THANK YOU." Melen repeated herself, swapping from Derik to Mirus and back again with her crushing hugs.

Derik sneaked a side-glance at a disgruntled Jeralin, the winning grin clearly showing on his face.

"Huh…there's always next year," Jeralin sneered, a slight roll in his eyes as he skulked back to his family waiting in the stands.

Derik, Mirus and Melene took to the stage as the administrator welcomed the trio. "The city's leadership is now bestowed upon Melene of the Wilkinson family." The administrator's announcement bringing brilliant smiles to Mirus and Derik's faces. Derik took a step forward and bowed arrogantly, winking at Jeralin in the crowd. Mirus placed her hand on the small of Melene's back, pushing her forward as the administrator presented a crown encrusted with darkened jewels that once belonged to Gandalin.

Melene held the crown high above her head, a smile of pride sweeping across her face as she gently placed it atop.

Mirus placed her hand on Derik's shoulder. "Well. You did it."

"Well. It was thanks to you I am here to see it." Derik said, staring deep into her eyes and taking hold of her hand. "Thank you.

"

"I can't believe all we got was this silly rock for risking life and limb for Melene," Derik grumbled, twirling an orange shimmering stone through his fingers. "I mean I could have died…actually, I did die," he said, tossing the stone to Mirus, who gracefully caught it.

"Derik. Don't you know what this is? Of course you don't. You would probably have just as much of an idea of what this stone can do than what Melene would have. We should be thanking our lucky stars she held on to this family heirloom for so long," Mirus' condescending tone so perfectly leaving her lips.

"It's an Ignis Charm." Before Derik could retort with his question about what an Ignis Charm is, Mirus continued. "This will shield the wearer from absolute heat. It should come in quite handy when we go through Fire Mountain. But before we head North, we need to get to my great grandfather's shrine."

"So how far away is this shrine?" Derik asked stopping to take a breath on a large white boulder by the path.

"It's not too far. We should get there just after sunrise. That is if we don't stop," Mirus said casually, walking on before Derik had a chance to reply.

Mirus unwrapped Argonus' staff, not missing a step as she continued forward with her eyes closed, waving it in small circles in front of her.

"What are you doing?" Derik asked curiously.

Mirus broke the silence with an alluring chant, "*Lūmen Ille Quasi.*"

The immediate area surrounding the two of them illuminating with a brilliant blue light.

Derik stood in amazement. "You're just full of surprises!" he said, bringing a smile to Mirus' face.

The farther they walked the more Derik's feet ached, making every step heavier than the last and he started to wonder if they should take a minute to rest.

"Perhaps we should set up and stay for the night," Mirus said, as if reading Derik's mind.

Derik smiled, "I couldn't agree more," he replied, sitting and rubbing his feet. Mirus held the staff high above her head. "*Finite*," she whispered. The light emanating from the staff was cut leaving them in the darkness of night as she handed the staff to Derik.

"*Tegmen.*" Mirus whispered, her arm glowing white as leaves, sticks and rocks surrounding them converged together, a small cave-like structure left behind as the white light faded. "We shall sleep here."

Darkness was still throwing shadows over the surrounding land as Derik's eyes adjusted, drenched in sweat from the dream that saw him once again witness his mother's demise. He sat upright, taking a moment for his mind to become clear, realising what this new day ahead was. He reached for a stick sitting close by and began drawing in the dirt, the scraping sound waking Mirus.

"What are you doing?" Mirus asked as she rolled over watching as Derik swirled the last light of a candle onto his drawing.

"I left Lūnam one year ago today. This is the day that 17 years ago I fell through the dome. Ranūl calls today my re-birthday." Derik said, taking a deep breath and blowing the flames of the candles inscribed in the ground away.

"Well then Derik, today is cause for celebration," Mirus' enthusiasm didn't appeal to Derik as he swivelled on the spot, taking to his feet and faced away from her.

"I'm not sure today is a day I wish to remember. I like to try and think that this is simply a normal day like any other. I just miss..." Derik was interrupted as Mirus dug her heels into the earth and spun, gripping Derik's forearm. Putting her finger to her lips to silence him before he could speak.

"Derik! Quickly over here. Someone is coming," Mirus whispered, gesturing for Derik to follow her behind a tree.

The two crouched low behind the tree watching intently in the direction the stone graunching noise was coming from and just as Mirus had said, four shadows emerged from the dark, shovelling their way past the tree in the direction that Mirus and Derik were headed.

"Did you get a good look at them?" Mirus asked once they were again alone.

"No, it was too dark. I could only see shadows."

"Well around these parts you cannot trust anyone, they could have been thieves," Mirus replied.

"Should we keep going?" Derik said with a nod.

"Yes, we are almost there," Mirus said, pointing toward the mountain range just ahead with the staff and chanting the illumination incantation to light their way once more.

CHAPTER 10

THE STONES OF EMPOWERMENT

If ever there were a paradise surely it was here. An untouched growth of forestry that snaked toward the tip of the mountain wall surrounding the duo, complemented a golden glittering path that sparkled off the still, crystal clear lake between them and the pass that Mirus assured Derik, would lead them directly to the shrine.

"Mirus, are you sure you know where we're going?" Derik's question contained a quiver of concern that Mirus may not know the shrine's exact location.

The crunch of footsteps on the stone path ahead of Derik stopped and Mirus swivelled briskly on her heels to face the absurd accusation face on. "Of course. I know where I'm going!" She snapped and twirled again, walking off in a huff.

Derik stood stunned for a moment before quickly reducing the distance between himself and Mirus. "Well, it's just we've been walking for half a day. And I kinda thought…" Derik trailed off as he realised Mirus had quickened her pace once again, before turning her head to remark derisively, "Derik. Be patient. We should arrive soon!"

"Hey, isn't this where the Regius live?" Derik asked reaching Mirus's side once more and deciding a new subject of discussion was in order to ease the tension.

"Yup. Vicious as they are cute. But only when they have been disturbed or threatened." Mirus' short and matter of fact response was softer than her previous tone.

A humour fuelled snort escaped Derik's nose, "Fuzzy little balls of terror!"

Derik and Mirus stood peering into the dense brush surrounding them, their faces reflecting one another's inquisitiveness. But the eerie silence was short lived and the duo's ears pricked at the approaching crunch of foliage, followed swiftly by the sudden appearance of a fuzzy ball of hair, teeth and claws whirling through the air towards Derik's head.

"DERIK! WATCH OUT," Mirus shouted swinging the crystal staff from her side and chanting '*Aequus.*'

A green spark flew from the tip of the staff, engulfing the Regius as it slid across the stone pathway, shifting its weight and gliding sideways in preparation for a second attack. As the green mana seeped deep into the little creature it stopped, almost frozen to the spot; the grunts and squeals which were previously echoing through the ranges no longer coming from the small ball of fur.

"What did you do to it?" Derik whispered, not wanting to draw the creature's attention.

"Well, there's no reason for them to be like this. I put a calming charm on him," Mirus replied, walking over to the completely placid Regius and swooping it into her arms.

Derik's eyes widened with shock. He couldn't believe that the creature that was just trying to kill them was now lazily lying in Mirus' arms.

"That's incredible. Why was it so frazzled? It's almost like it was after blood."

Mirus looked back at Derik with a look of great concern. "This one's been spooked. Someone else has been through here. It must have been those noisy goons that walked past us last night," Mirus said placing the Regius back on the path and watching it slowly scuttle back into the foliage.

"Should we keep going?" Derik asked gesturing for Mirus to lead the way.

Mirus didn't reply. She was completely still with her eyes staring into the distance, then speedily put her hand up to stop Derik.

"Is there something wrong?" Derik asked, breaking the silence.

Mirus remained silent, simply lifting a finger to her lips commanding quiet.

Derik strained his ears listening to the silence but heard only that, silence. It was a few moments before Mirus finally spoke.

"Did you hear that?"

"Hear what?" Derik replied.

"I heard voices and laughter"

"Mirus, I think you might need to rest. I didn't hear a thing."

"No. I know what I heard Derik!"

Mirus stepped onto the soft earth by the stony path and began creeping forward cautiously, rounding a corner that opened into a bare stone clearing with a cave at the far side.

"That's it. That's the shrine," Mirus said excitedly, the noises she'd heard earlier seeming to have left her mind.

Derik grinned an awkward smile and took a deep breath to clear his mind of the impending change that was about to be bestowed upon him.

"Shall we?" Mirus said gesturing for Derik to enter the cave.

Derik began walking across the stone path toward the cavern opening, coming to a halt as four figures became visible in the shadows of the cave's entrance.

"Huh, lookey who we have here," came a deep voice from one of the shadows that rang familiar to Derik.

The four figures stepped out from the cover of the shadows. Derik felt his blood pumping with a slight anger, letting shock take over as he noticed that it was Xardos and three of the Halflings from the Metaprep.

"What are you doing in my great grandfather's shrine?" Mirus yelled across to them.

"We heard that there was a shrine hidden in the Regius Ranges," said one of the creature men. "And in this shrine were three of the most precious stones in the world," interrupted another. "But we only found one," the last beast grunted, shoving the one who had spoken before him.

"As I understand it, these three stones are told to bring great power to the person that possesses all three," Xardos said taking a step toward the duo; throwing a glowing yellow stone into the air above his head and letting it fall back into his hand, a smirk growing across his thin face.

Derik turned to Mirus, who looked as though she was about to explode with anger.

"GIVE THAT BACK! It doesn't belong to you," Mirus screamed, stepping forward with her fist raised.

"And who's going to make me? You and your pathetic little friend," Xardos' condescending tone echoed through the surrounds as he and the rest of the gang burst into a deep laughter.

Derik looked from the gang and back to Mirus again, still recovering from the shock his body had forced him into. Mirus slid her feet together and swayed the staff from right to left letting out an almighty bellow; "*Incendere Globus.*"

A great red fireball flew from the staff and hit the ground at Xardos' feet, the force knocking him backwards.

"*Mysticus Advocō Prōtinus,*" Mirus followed, raising the staff high in the air.

A blinding flash of light filled the area surrounding them and when Derik opened his eyes a familiar scene lay before him. Mirus had conjured a Mystic, but what Xardos and his gang didn't know was it was a mere illusion.

"Drop the stone and leave, or I won't hesitate to feed my friend here," Mirus said nodding toward the Mystic, a deep rumble following the cloud of smoke that puffed from its nose.

The entire gang was frozen in place with their eyes fixed on the great mythical beast.

Mirus commanded the Mystic to move toward Xardos. Quivering on the spot, he let go of his grip on the stone, allowing it fall to the ground and ran from the clearing, the gang following close behind.

When Derik and Mirus could no longer hear their screams of terror, Mirus returned the Mystic with another swift flick of the staff and the duo burst into laughter.

"Did you see the looks on their faces?" Derik said catching his breath and clutching his chest.

Mirus straightened herself. "Yes…it was very much the same look you had on your face back in the Forest of Night." Derik stuck out his tongue at her patronising response, walking to the cave entrance and retrieving the yellow stone from the ground. "Well, I guess I'm not the only one that fell for that one," he said shooting Mirus a mischievous smile.

"And I had plenty more where that came from if they were willing to try me," Mirus replied showing a slightly malicious side that Derik had not seen in her before.

As Derik entered the shrine, close behind Mirus, he was surprised to see it was akin to the inside of a vast palace more so than the inner earthly look he was expecting. Rugs hung from the walls and the entire shrine was lit with a soft glow from burning torches staked into the ground around the room. But when Derik's eyes fell across the centrepiece the uneasy feeling in the pit of his stomach returned as he remembered the reason they were there.

"That is where the stones need to be placed," Mirus said, walking to the large rock in the centre of the room where three small crevices were carved into the face.

Derik walked over and stood by Mirus' side, reaching over to the centrepiece to place the yellow stone in the first gap when Mirus suddenly gripped his arm tightly, holding him in place.

"They must be fitted in the correct order. You can't just go shoving them in, in any order or it won't work," Mirus said condescendingly, snatching the stone from Derik.

"And I guess you know which order to put them in then?" Derik replied, a tremor of sarcasm rippling through his words.

"Of course I do. The right combination, if I remember correctly, is red, yellow and then blue."

Mirus took the red stone from the bracelet Derik had given her and reached out for Derik's necklace.

"We will need that," she said, holding out her hand.

Derik took hold of the gem hanging from his neck, his heart beating erratically in his chest at the thought of handing over the last physical object that linked to the memory of his mother.

"Ok, but be careful," he said, reluctantly coiling the chain into Mirus' hand.

"Derik you should stand over there," Mirus pointed to a circle etched into the floor in front of the centrepiece.

Derik breathed deeply, holding it in. His heavy and slow steps exposed his reluctance as he reached the centre of the circle, swivelling on one foot to face Mirus as she placed the last stone into its opening.

"Now, I need you to repeat after me. This is the mantra that you need to say in order for the re-empowerment to be successful," said Mirus, an odd longing gleam resonating from her eyes.

"*Contrā Illē Trēs*," Mirus chanted.

"*Contrā Illē Trēs,*" Derik imitated, but the words seemed to flow from his lips as if he knew the mantra by heart.

"*Lapis Solvere Ille Retinēre Potestās.*"

Mirus' mouth slowly closed as Derik finished repeating the enchantment. As the sound of the final syllable died, the room began to shake, small pieces of rock falling from the ceiling and knocking both Derik and Mirus to their knees. Derik made a desperate attempt to crawl for the cave entrance before the roof caved them in but a barrier that was not visible was keeping him confined to the circle. He scrambled to his feet and thumped on the walls of the invisible enclosure. Mirus sat watching as small flashes of blue electric streaks of light repeatedly struck Derik, and as swiftly as it had started the shaking came to a halt.

Mirus jumped to her feet and rushed to Derik's side as he lay motionless on the floor.

Placing her hand on his arm she forcefully nudged him, the desperate look matching her tone. "Derik! Derik!!! Are you alright?"

A dusting of sand blew from the front of Derik's mouth as he breathed a moan.

He slowly got to his feet and forced an awkward smile.

"Yeah, I think so. Did it work?" he asked hoping he hadn't gone through the brutal pain he had endured for nothing.

"Only you would know. Ah...try something from this," Mirus said, reaching into her pocket and handing Derik a few pieces of folded parchment and the staff. "These are all the incantations that my great grandfather knew. He crafted most of them on his own."

Derik took the parchment and read one of the spells aloud.

"*Incendere Globus.*" The deep voice Derik put on as he lifted his shoulders back in an attempt to look and sound more powerful was short lived. Nothing happened.

"I don't understand. It should have worked, even if you were being ridiculous about it," Mirus mocked.

"Maybe I just need time to grow into it or something."

"I guess only time will tell. Well, the Valley of Mystics calls Derik. We should go. I am sure we will have you using your mana in no time." Mirus' reassurance somewhat lifting Derik's spirits as the two flashed each other a determined smile.

CHAPTER 11

KEEPER OF LIGHT

"I've never seen clouds like that before! What do you suppose that is?" Derik asked, raising an eyebrow at the forest ahead.

Mirus followed Derik's gaze and was struck with the same question. Hovering close to the canopy of the lightly glowing forest, an expanding cloak of deepening clouds paraded a drizzle of despair through the trees.

"I can't be sure … but they don't have much resemblance to regular storm-clouds," Mirus replied stopping to climb on the stub of a fallen tree to get a better look. "That's the Forest of Light and it should most certainly not be swathed in darkness."

"I've heard that name before. Ranūl told me of stories from his past travels. He used to come here long ago to purify his spirit and trade for light crystals. It doesn't look too inviting right now though," Derik shrugged at the thought. "Whatever it is, it will have to wait," he continued with a little smile on his face flipping his pack from his shoulder and tearing a few pages of parchment into pieces, throwing them within a small stone circle he had prepared on the ground.

"I suppose it can wait. Yes, for now we rest!" Mirus struggled with her decision, but after a moment in thought she nudged Derik aside and pointed the staff toward the stone circle, her incantation setting fire to the pieces of parchment and branches Derik had gathered; a sight that he was only just beginning to get used to.

Mirus took a seat by the now billowing flames and Derik took out two loaves of Marland, handing one to Mirus.

"Mirus," he spluttered through his first mouthful, "Is it just me, or does the forest look like it's getting darker?"

As the storm clouds assembled themselves into a growing darkened mass, the glowing light that looked as though it was emanating from the essence of the forest itself was slowly beginning to fade.

Mirus's forehead wrinkled with deep lines of concern. "We are definitely going to have to see what's going on once we wake." No question of great urgency in her voice.

The early morning dew was building on the blades of grass surrounding the spot Derik had chosen to rest for the night. He rubbed his eyes and sat up adjusting to the low light and was surprised to see Mirus huddled on the tree stub watching the forest in the distance.

"It has only been getting worse. I think we should go to it," Mirus said quietly and rather urgently as Derik reached her side.

"Have you been up all night?" he asked, stretching out a relieving yawn.

"We must leave immediately," she replied, gracefully floating from the stump to the ground and hurrying ahead.

Sometimes Mirus was a little too mysterious for Derik's liking. He never liked it when Ranūl had kept things from him as a boy, yet somehow Mirus reminded him of his adopted carer. He felt comfortable with her, safe. Over time, he had come to the conclusion that this was a good thing too, as he stood staring into a familiar scene at the entrance of the dark pathway into the forest.

"It looks like the Forest of Night in there."

It seemed as though Mirus had not heard the words he had just uttered but she turned sternly, her response filled with apprehension. "This is very strange! This isn't normal at all. It should be flooded with light, not shadowed darkness. Something is most certainly not right here."

Derik lunged forward and snatched the staff from Mirus, raising it in the air, "No worries," he smirked, "I'll just use a spell to light our way." Derik closed his eyes tightly in concentration and chanted the words, '*Lūmen Ille Quasi.*' He opened his eyes hoping to see the area flooded with light, but realising the spell hadn't worked he lowered his head in disappointment. Mirus reached her hand out for the staff, flashing Derik an apologetic wince as she repeated the illuminating incantation. A bright white light flooded the area around them.

"I don't understand why it didn't work." The disappointment getting the better of him as he lifted his head to Mirus and frowned.

Mirus put her hand on Derik's shoulder. "It will come to you Derik, you just need to concentrate and learn to control the power that is within you," she said, turning the staff toward the darkened forest.

"Well at least *you* have solved our problem," Derik's sarcastic tone brought a triumphant smile to Mirus' face, which didn't last long once she turned back to the forest.

"Yes, but it doesn't solve theirs!" Mirus exclaimed, pointing to a stone statue that resembled one of the forest's Light Workers.

Derik stepped through the broken branches littering the forest floor and tapped the tip of the Light Worker's nose. "It looks so real, like it was alive!"

"That's because it is...well was," Mirus replied as she joined Derik next to the stone statue. "Something must have happened to the Keeper of Light. The pure essence that flows between the Keeper and the forest must be broken," she said running her hand along the Light Worker's back.

"Who or what is the Keeper of Light?" Derik wondered aloud.

"The Keeper of Light is the forest's spirit guide. It chooses a physical host whose primary path becomes to ensure the balance of energetic purity within the forest. He has a sanctuary in the centre of the forest; I think we should go and see him," Mirus said leading the way.

Through the darkness Derik could detect the faintest smell of needles from the pine oaks and the purity of the air filled his lungs with joy through every breath, when suddenly an uncomfortably sweet scent filled his nostrils.

"Wow, what is *that*? Do you smell it?" Derik blurted out suddenly describing the heavenly yet disturbing scent. But Mirus didn't seem to share his likeness to the smell, screwing up her nose and immediately beginning to search the area, muttering to herself.

"Mirus, what are you looking for?" Derik asked joining her in the search for an item he was yet to know about, when the light from the staff passed over a motionless body lying face down.

"Mirus, there's someone over there," Derik uttered urgently as he noticed that the person the light had passed by was barely breathing.

"It's a Light Worker, and he's hurt." Mirus raced to the battered body on the forest floor and knelt beside him and placed the staff on the forest floor.

"Hey," Mirus whispered as she gently shook the Light Worker, "Are you alright? Say something if you can hear me!"

Mirus leaned in close to hear the fading whisper. "Watch for..." the Light Worker spluttered, cringing in pain but pushing to finish his sentence. "The... the shadows," he choked.

"What did he say?" Derik asked looking from the Light Worker and back to Mirus.

"He said 'watch for the shadows.' I'm not sure exactly what he means," Mirus replied, turning back to the injured man. "It's alright we're going to help you okay. This may sting a little but please hold as still as you can," she whispered closing her eyes and holding her hands clapped together over his centre. A few moments passed and she turned to Derik worry stricken.

"I cannot heal him. His body is in too much of a bad state."

Derik frowned as he looked desperately at Mirus. "Surely there is something we ca..." Derik's words trailed off as he raised his eyebrows in excitement and flipped his pack from his shoulder, scrambling around within.

"What are you doing?" Mirus asked.

Derik gleamed as he removed a small bottle containing a clear liquid from his pack.

"I only have a little left, but it should be enough," he said as he leant down and dribbled the last of the Phoenix Tears onto the large wound on the Light Worker's side. A small waft of blue floated from the gash as the Light Worker's skin weaved itself back together.

Derik and Mirus each took an arm, helping the Light Worker gently to his feet. He let go and wobbled as he regained his balance, brushing his light chainmail vest. His shoulder length, silver hair reflected the light of the staff as his pale skin returned to full colour. "Thank you, I don't know what I would have done had you not come along. I shall be sworn by your side 'til my debt is repaid. My name is Ilaseon," he said, one arm behind his back as he bowed to the duo.

Derik put out his hand, "I'm Derik and this is Mirus."

Ilaseon took Derik's hand and shook it with a smile of gratitude.

"You said something as you lay on the floor...'watch for the shadows.' What is it that you meant by that?" Mirus asked, taking additional care not to step out of the light from the staff.

"The shadows of those who have passed are arising from their place of rest. They were once Elanore's followers and can feel her essence drawing stronger," Ilaseon answered. "They were headed towards the Keeper of Light's sanctuary. We must hurry."

Derik let out a short laugh. "Ha, I don't think that Elanore is drawing any nearer," Derik said as he pulled out the half stone he possessed, "Both pieces need to be joined together for that, right!?"

Fear spread across Ilaseon's face as he noticed what Derik was holding.

"Fool. You cannot hold that out in the open. *They* will see it," Ilaseon said snatching the stone from Derik's hands and swiftly shoving it into his own pocket.

Derik fell silent, standing stiffly with his head bowed, entirely still.

"Derik?" Ilaseon called out, his eyes darting from the dark forest surrounding them and back to Derik.

"Ohh, thisss one is ssstrong," an unfamiliar voice croaked from Derik's mouth as he looked up to face Ilaseon and Mirus. "Yesss, our Queen will be pleasssed," he followed, a dark smile creeping across his face.

Mirus inched toward Derik with her arms raised slightly. "Derik, what are you talking about? Maybe you should come and sit down," she said reaching for his arm.

"Nnnoo, we will not be ssstopped," the voice crackled again from Derik's lips, as he turned to face Ilaseon.

"You... I wantsss that stone." A darker tone escaping Derik's lips this time.

"I will give it back when it is safe to, after we seek out The Keeper," Ilaseon replied.

"Noooww," Derik bellowed, his voice echoing through the dark lifeless forest.

Mirus reached out again and placed her hand on Derik's shoulder, "Derik, you know what could happen if the spirits were to get their hands on it," she said.

Derik turned stiffly to face Mirus and without hesitation he swiftly swung his arm throwing her to the ground, turning back to Ilaseon and leaping for his throat. Mirus got to her feet brushing the twigs from her dress and raced over to where the two lay struggling on the ground. "Derik, stop this madness. What has come over you?" She managed to splutter out.

Derik turned his head awkwardly, lifted his hand towards Mirus and screeched "*Navitas Pila*."

A great electric blue ball of energy crackled from Derik's palm and struck Mirus.

As the open opportunity presented itself to him, Ilaseon quickly reacted knocking the distracted Derik face first to the ground, leaping onto his back.

"Derik! *Please*! You mustn't look into darkness; you'll shine brighter without it. Fight it Derik!" he whispered.

Mirus groaned as she lifted herself to her feet, rubbing her head where she had collided with a tree. Hearing Ilaseon's words gave her an idea.

"Here goes nothing. '*Abesse ab malus anima, abesse ab,*'" she chanted.

Derik again turned his head awkwardly to the side and started shrieking in a high-pitched tone, clamping his skull with his hands.

Ilaseon slowly backed away in fear of his life, just in time to avoid a dark static stream of smoke sprouting from Derik's mouth that vanished into the darkness of the forest. Mirus slowly approached Derik as he lay still on the forest floor. "Derik. Are you alright?"

Derik moaned, raising his arm to haul himself off the ground and Ilaseon and Mirus watched as he got to his feet, looking around in confusion.

"What just happened?" he asked, rubbing a spot on his knee that was mysteriously hurting.

"One of the shadows... the spirits... must have possessed you. We are lucky to be alive. Your body displayed itself to be a very dangerous yet powerful vessel," Ilaseon explained, "From now on we have to be extra careful."

Mirus nodded her head in agreement and turned to Derik, "That spell you used was not one of Argonus'. That was one Elanore used frequently during her reign to frighten the people of Altāsia to follow her. I fear that we will endure more of this erratic behaviour from many of the land's creatures and the spirits who watch over it, but I am glad you are alright," she said turning to Ilaseon, "And just for safe keeping I think I should hold onto the stone. I will not be overcome by these spirits so easily."

Ilaseon reached into his pocket and handed the half stone to Mirus. "Yes. Of course. Please, take it."

"Thank you," she replied as she put it into her pocket, sealing it shut with a quick wave of the staff. "Now to the sanctuary, to see The Keeper," she said gesturing for Derik and Ilaseon to follow suit.

Questions grew in Derik's mind as they walked. He could not stand the uncertainty and decided to blurt them out to break the silence.

"Ilaseon, what will happen if the spirits become resurrected?"

"Well at first, as we just saw, they will seek out the two halves of the stone," Ilaseon replied, "Then they will release Elanore and continue along her side from where they left off; a quest for destruction and domination."

Derik looked at the ground then back to Ilaseon and nodded in understanding.

"We won't have to worry about that if we get to the sanctuary in time to stop them," Mirus added, as they stepped into an open clearing with a grand bluestone-building centrepiece.

"We must be on our sharpest alert," Ilaseon whispered as he crept to the doorway and entered the blackened sanctuary.

Mirus and Derik shot a sharp nod at one another and with a quick 'Finite' the light from the staff faded and they too entered the doorway.

The inside of the sanctuary was shadowed in darkness, but for a tiny luminous glimmer at the far side of the room.

"There he is," Mirus whispered to Derik.

"Yes, but where are the spirits? That's what I'm worried about!" Derik replied, straining to see through the darkness.

The trio slowly approached the lightly glowing figure that lay motionless on the floor.

"I believe we are too late!" Ilaseon said as he crouched down beside The Keeper of Light, "They have taken his life force. There is now nothing we can do to help him."

"Does that mean that the *Followers* are living again?" Derik asked shuffling closer to Mirus and reaching for the staff.

"Derik, don't do anything that will attract attention!" Mirus said. But she was too late; no sooner than Mirus had given the warning Derik had snatched the staff from her grasp and called out, *"Lūmen Ille Quasi,"* the whole room illuminating for a moment before dying back to darkness.

The quivering voice of Ilaseon came from the darkness, "Please tell me I wasn't the only one who just saw that."

"No. I saw it too," Mirus whispered as she snatched the staff back from Derik's grasp and swung it in the dark, lighting the room with a brilliant light.

Mirus, Derik and Ilaseon stood in the now light flooded room, staring into the eyes of ten unsightly looking spirits.

"Well, What *doo* we have here?" One of the hovering shadows of Elanore's Followers screeched to the others.

"I bags the Light Worker," another replied.

"We need to do something before we end up like the Light Keeper over there," Derik said gesturing towards the faded body in the room's corner.

"We cannot let them do this. The end of the world is *nigh*," Ilaseon quivered in a state of panic.

Derik turned to Mirus for support and as the light from the incantation began to fade, he noticed she had her eyes closed, head down and hands clamped together.

"Mirus?" Derik called in confusion, but instead of a reply Mirus flung open her eyes, lifted her hands toward the floating shadowed figures and screamed "*Dīmittere*."

As the word flowed from her mouth the ten spirits that stood in front of them transformed one by one into small circular shaped pods and floated through the ceiling.

"What was *that*?" Derik asked.

"That was '*sending*' ten evil spirits to their final resting place!" Mirus replied falling to her knees from exhaustion.

"But I thought that once draining The Keeper's life force they were alive again!"

Ilaseon reached out a hand and placed it on Derik's shoulder. "There must have been too many of them trying to feed from the one life force, so it seems they only took a portion each and could not gain a physical form, only regain their original shape!" he explained.

"What about him?" Derik asked Ilaseon pointing to the motionless body on the sanctuary floor.

"I don't know? This has never happened in my time!" he replied.

Mirus turned to Ilaseon and explained, "This has happened once before! If I remember correctly the spirit guide will choose the next Keeper through The Keeper's crown."

Derik walked over and picked up the crown that lay on the floor by the grey, motionless body of the former Keeper and placed upon his head. "Nothing," he said as he turned to Ilaseon, "Here, you try!"

"No-one but The Keeper has ever laid a hand on the crown before, I'm not sure I should," he said, his eyes wide with concern.

Ilaseon let out a small squeak reluctantly taking the crown from Derik, placing it upon his own head.

A glow of pure light began to emanate brightly from the crown, circling Ilaseon from the top of his head and snaking its way around his body to the ground. Beneath his feet, the earth radiated with a light that began to extend outward. The forest surrounding the sanctuary burst into light and sounds of life slowly refilled the silence.

CHAPTER 12

FOUNTAIN OF TEARS

Derik couldn't help but notice Mirus was still finding it hard to stay on her feet and seeing her occasional sway from side-to-side had him prepared to catch her, if she were to lose the battle with gravity. Reaching up to place a hand on her shoulder to steady her for the moment, Derik walked her to a stump by the grand stone pillars marking the entrance to The Keeper of Light's sanctuary and sat beside her.

"You look strung out. Maybe Ilaseon has a place you can rest before we continue," he said gesturing toward the new Keeper in hope that he would offer before she was to ask.

Picking up on Derik's subtlety Ilaseon fumbled forward announcing that she would replenish faster if she took respite in the meditation room inside the shrine. Mirus nodded sluggishly as she plopped to her feet and managed to slog her way back into the shrine where she lay to rest on the sweet scented floor, curling up in the soft roots of an ancient oak tree growing out through the wall of the meditation room.

"You are too, more than welcome to replenish," Ilaseon gestured to Derik once Mirus was out of sight. But there was no way Derik could sleep with all of the conflicting thoughts that raced through his mind. He could feel the energies building deep within and the fact that a spirit had chosen to possess him earlier because it too felt the power growing within him, troubled Derik.

He wasn't sure how long he had been sitting in thought when suddenly his concentration was interrupted as a springy Mirus skipped through the sanctuary doorway.

"You look better!" He complemented Mirus with a smile.

"I feel much better! Amazing actually! Where did Ilaseon go?" she replied, noticing Derik was sitting alone.

Scouring the surrounding forest quickly in confusion Derik shrugged. "I'm not sure? He was here just a moment ago," he replied, uncertainty vibrating through his words as he realised he was so deep in thought he hadn't noticed Ilaseon leave. Getting to his feet Derik walked to Mirus' side and the two called into the depths of the forest in hope he was still nearby. After a few minutes of silence, the duo assumed he had left to heal the rest of the forest; a task that had now become his life long quest as the new Keeper of Light.

"I would have liked to thank him for his hospitality, but we really must continue Derik!" Mirus said leading the way North.

Nightfall had taken the land and as they pushed on through last of the dense undergrowth of the Forest of Light, Derik again began trying to focus on the powerful, expanding sensations that pulsed from deep within his body.

He concentrated his thoughts while they walked, searching the control of his inner power for some kind of connection with the mana and as he pulled at the consciousness deep inside, a shudder reverberated through his body sending a jolt of blue sparks outwards from below his chest.

"You'll need to stop doing that!" Mirus uttered, leaping out of the way, yet again, as another blueish crack frizzed from Derik's middle.

"Sorry," he grinned sheepishly. "I am trying, but this energy... the mana...seems to have a mind of its own!"

"You need to focus," Mirus stated as a matter of fact, pausing and suddenly grasping Derik by the shoulders, turning him to face her. "You have to control it or it will control you...HEY!" She leapt to one side as another jagged blue light zipped toward the earth and a small plant that had been struck began to smoke rapidly, bursting into flames.

"Sorry." A more sincere apology escaping Derik's lips this time.

"Try breathing into the energy," suggested Mirus, standing further away now and eyeing him warily. "Calm it down a bit and perhaps use this as a conduit," she said, handing Derik the staff.

Derik nodded understandingly and began breathing in and out slowly and consciously as he took hold of the staff, holding it tightly with both hands. He felt his insides flutter as the spark began to build and tried to imagine it contained and quiet.

Recalling one of the spells on the parchment Mirus had given him earlier he let go as he slowly exhaled, feeling the energy push through his arms and into the staff. "*Igniculus.*"

A surge of power sparked from the staff and struck the visible roots of the exact tree he had been focusing on. A smug smile crept across his face. He looked to Mirus, who was standing with her hands on her hips and he raised his eyebrows questioningly and she shrugged back in response seemingly unimpressed.

"Better, I guess," she said. "Just remind me not to stand next to you in the rain."

Derik rolled his eyes and sighed loudly. "Well, I thought it was a good effort," he said, nudging Mirus in the shoulder as he pushed past her, continuing North toward the final area of Altāsia between them and the Valley of Mystics, Fire Mountains.

A sudden burst of heat lit up the early morning sky as the mountain tops erupted in front of them, sending plumes of scarlet fire shooting high into the air. Taking a few paces forward, Derik cringed at the narrow winding path curving its way high into the mountains but his focus quickly shifted to a grand blood red Phoenix statue marking the path's beginning. Suspended in mid-air beneath the feet of the Phoenix, glowing words glittered and shone through the new day's fading dark.

Mirus was mouthing the words silently to herself and looked up at the imposing statue staring impassively ahead.

"From the ashes of fire, we shall be reborn through the flames of life. It's talking about the Phoenix, right?" Derik said, half to himself and half to Mirus, although he didn't really expect a reply.

The path was steep and with each step Derik found himself struggling for breath. It wasn't just the altitude getting to him, the heat was beginning to become unbearable as they journeyed deeper through the fiery plumes for which the mountains were named.

Mirus indicated for him to stop and she leaned forward, falling to her hands on her knees, her breathing erratic and loud.

"Are you ok?" Derik asked taking a step toward her. The doubled-up figure made a sound he took to be a yes. Mirus straightened up and not realising just how close Derik was, instinctively took a step backwards, her heel slipping over the edge of the mountain pathway. Derik shot out an arm to grab her. "Careful," he cried, pulling her sharply into his arms.

"Thanks. That was close," she replied gratefully, her chest continuing to heave with the effort to breathe. Mirus released herself from Derik's grip and reached a hand to her forehead, wiping away beads of sweat.

"Phew...Hot enough for you?"

"Wait...where is the Ignis Charm? That should help us right?" Derik smiled at Mirus' reaction as she rolled her eyes, flicked her wrist to reveal her pocket and removing the orange stone.

"I can't believe I had forgotten about this and what I am even more surprised about is the fact that *you* remembered," she retorted, tapping the Ignis Charm three times to activate its ability to protect the bearer from heat.

"What about me?" Derik replied, wiping the beads of sweat that had dripped from his forehead down his cheeks.

"I was getting to that," Mirus replied, taking hold of Derik's hand.

"What are you doing?" His already heat blushed cheeks growing a little brighter

"Well, so long as I have hold of your hand, the charm will flow across to the both of us," Mirus said. "And don't worry Derik, I'm just as unhappy about this as you are." Mirus' words left Derik feeling uncomfortable.

"Have you noticed there's nothing growing here?" he asked, hoping to ease the tension. "No insects either."

"Well I suppose it's not a paradise for anything living," replied Mirus

"I just can't believe how quiet it is though...aside from the bursts of flames from the mountains that is," he replied, searching the pathway ahead for any signs of life.

"We must almost be through the mountains," she began to explain. "They say the closer you get to the North end, there is only but the dust and the heat, rumoured to have driven the bravest of men mad!" she added as another streak of flames arced through the inky sky.

"I guess there's no going back now," said Derik with a wry smile. Mirus smiled back briefly and then looked ahead to the length of pathway that still stretched out before them. "Upwards and onwards."

As they drudged through the final few meters, a strong sense they were being watched washed through Derik like a disorderly storm and a sudden energy surge overcame what control he had managed to muster; a bright blue streak crackling from his hands making rubble out of a nearby mountain wall.

"Woah...careful Derik, there isn't much room on this path remember." Mirus snapped. "You need to learn how to stop doing that now anyway," she added, her face wrinkling in exasperation.

"Ahh! Sorry I lost control...There's something out there watching us," Derik said, looking desperately around. "I can't explain. I can just feel it?"

Mirus nodded. "It's Elanore's Qi," she said simply. "She's growing stronger."

"Do you think that's what I'm feeling?" he replied.

"I'm sure of it. You know, while we've been walking, I've been thinking. I believe the only way we can destroy Elanore once and for all is if we bring the two halves of the stone together and release her, then..."

"WHAT?" cried Derik. "Mirus, are you completely insane?" His eyes were blazing as he threw Mirus' hand away from his own. "We can't do that. Isn't it too much of a risk?" His torso fizzed and crackled as sparks flew off in all directions.

They stood facing each other on the narrow path, both of them tense with irritation. "Don't call me insane!" Mirus snapped back.

"Well, it's a pretty stupid idea, isn't it?"

"Fine! You come up with something better then," she shouted, letting out a short sharp snarl and walking back down the path, her hands balled into fists.

Derik waited until she was out of sight and needing to release some of the pent-up frustration, he began to climb the small rock face to his left. He stopped to sit atop a small boulder halfway up the mountain and looked toward the direction

Mirus had stormed off in. He spotted her further down the path, sitting with her back to him and sighed. '*At least she hadn't left completely*' he thought, but they were arguing over nothing, it was insignificant considering the dangers they were surely soon to confront.

He closed his eyes tightly and then opened them again, swivelling around to face the wall behind him as beads of sweat once again began running down his forehead. '*Oh no! Mirus took the Ignis Charm with her,*' he thought, wiping the sweat with the back of his hand and flicking it on the wall in front of him. As he stared at the drops quickly evaporating from the heat, he turned his attention to a small crack in the rock face. "What the...?" he questioned aloud, curiosity getting the better of him immediately, as it always did. He got to his feet and after a little investigative probing, squeezed through the small gap.

"Well at least it's a little cooler in here." His relieved voice reverberating through the darkness ahead as he shuffled his way deeper into the tightly closed-in cavern. As the tight cave system widened a faint bubbling drip echoed ahead.

"Water! There's water in here?" He said excitedly, squeezing out from the tight tunnel and into a roomy cave

Illuminated by plumes of fire high in the ceiling of the cave, the sparkling fountain in the room caught Derik's attention. The shimmering refractions of firelight bounced off the walls of the cavern as if the cave itself was alive.

Derik noticed a tattered sign on the far side of the fountain and walked around behind the splashing cascade to read it

'Fountain Of Tears. Venturers Beware! Only those who possess a pure spirit can take from the lake.'

Not really reading the words, Derik realised how thirsty he was and he leaned forward, tempted by the crystal clear, pure water. As he cupped his hands to dip into the pool, a heart rending screech from above shattered the cave's tranquillity.

The cavern darkened as a great red and gold Phoenix plummeted through an opening just below the fiery ceiling, squirming and snapping at its back as it fell. Derik leapt out of the way, sliding across the floor as the normally majestic bird crashed heavily to the ground and smashed into the wall opposite him.

As it lay panting and squirming, a small scaly Graemol leaped from its back and lunged towards the bird's throat. Derik reached out his hand, panic exploding through his body sending several sparks of blue lightning into the cave's walls, floor, ceiling and striking the Graemol. With a shrill squeal of pain, the small creature was flung against the stone walls of the cave and bounced towards the cavern entrance. Scrambling to its feet it hobbled from the cave still emitting a quivering scream.

Derik stood unable to move, his fingers stinging from the electricity he had produced. He lowered his arm, a flash of red seeping through a tear in his shirt sleeve catching his attention as he realised he must have scraped it on the way through the tunnel into the cave. The Phoenix slowly rose from the ground and began heaving towards him, its head held high as if still trying to retain its pride after the attack. In a swift dipping motion, it wiped its moist eye on Derik's wound. The scrape pulsed warmly as the tears began to soak into his skin, burning briefly as it healed.

The bird turned and fixed a grateful, liquid amber gaze on Derik for a moment and slowly stretched its wings wide, taking off from the floor and out of the hole it had entered from. A sudden realisation washed over Derik as it occurred to him that the fountain was not filled with water, rather it was a fountain of Phoenix tears. He once again approached the fountain, bending down to reach into his pack that lay on the floor. He removed his own bottle that once contained Phoenix tears and dipped the bottle into the fountain, submerging it fully until it was once again full.

"Ha. Some warning," he whispered realising nothing had happened when he 'took from the lake.'

His thoughts began to wander and Mirus' plan to defeat Elanore eased back into his mind. '*Maybe she was right. Maybe it was the only way.*' He thought. He knew she couldn't do it without him and perhaps it really was his destiny to finally destroy Elanore.

"Hey!" he heard Mirus' frantic voice echoing down the crack he had come in through. "Derik! Where are you?"

"I'm fine. Over here!" He shouted back.

Mirus appeared squeezing into the opened cave. "I saw you go behind the boulder and come in here and then a Graemol came screaming out...followed by a Phoenix. I thought something might have happened to you...a..and...Oh, are you sure you're ok?"

Derik smiled at her. "I'm sure," he said. "I had a slight encounter with a Phoenix. The Graemol was attacking it so I zapped it!"

"You zapped it? Huh. That explains the screaming," said Mirus, looking relieved. "Listen Derik, I'm sorry about earlier. It was probably a stupid idea. You were quite right to..."

"No," interrupted Derik. "It's me that should apologise. You're right. I understand now what we need to do. And I will be here by your side every step of the way Mirus. We'll defeat Elanore. The two of us. We'll do it!"

Mirus gave his arm a little squeeze. "It rests my spirit to hear you say that. Thank you Derik," she whispered. "Now come on, let's get out of here."

The duo walked and climbed the remainder of the mountain path in amiable silence, both pleased that their quarrel was over and that they were united again in their determination to put a stop to Elanore once and for all.

The land lightened with the dawn sun's rays brightening the sky with pink and gold as they stood on the far side of the mountains.

"Look," Mirus finally said pointing into the distance.

A small island lay just offshore, its green and grey hills slowly emerging from the darkness of the falling night as the sun's rays washed over them. It was beautiful, peaceful even, with not a hint of the dangers that awaited there.

CHAPTER 13
AWAKENING

Derik's fingers curled around a handful of stones and threw them one-by-one into the sea, droplets of water from the splash rebounding back and landing on the shore's edge. He sighed heavily. "Valley of Mystics! Great, but how are we going to get there? It's too far to swim."

"There is a way," Mirus crossed her arms. "But only the two of us working together can achieve it, and I don't think you are quite ready yet."

Derik's arms flopped to his side. "What do you mean I'm not ready? I can handle anything."

Mirus rolled her eyes at Derik's stubborn and smug reply, a smirk creeping across her face, knowing quite well he was not ready to fulfill his part of the energy transfer needed. "Well then Derik, we shall try."

"What do I need to do?" Derik stood chest out, shoulders back and head high with confidence.

"This is no easy task Derik, and you are going to need to blend with the staff in order for this to work. As a matter of fact, that is going to be what you need when we are up against Elanore."

Derik's eyebrows wrinkled and his stance of confidence dropped. "And what exactly do I need to do to 'blend' with the staff Mirus? I mean it's not like we have months ahead of us, the Valley of Mystics is right there. And we both know that Xardos is probably already waiting," Derik said gesturing toward the island that was just out of reach.

Mirus sighed and took a step forward, taking Derik's hands. "You have already proven your connection to the staff, now you just need to master it and become whole. It's just as the old saying goes, the more you practice something the better you get at it."

"Ok Mirus. Show me how it is done," Derik said, conceding his own defeat of confidence and releasing his hands from Mirus' grip.

"Alright," Mirus replied, a wicked smile growing across her face, sending waves of concern through Derik's mind. "But just so you know, once I have taught you what you need to know, the blending will be up to you, and I won't be going easy on you."

'*Going easy on me, what is she talking about?*' Derik's concern was written all over his face.

Mirus took several steps back, her feet standing just along the land's edge. "First we need to master balance," she said, nodding her head to the side letting Derik know she wanted him to join her. Derik quickly skipped to her side turning to face the tips of Fire Mountain that towered beyond the path they had travelled.

Mirus held her arm outstretched, opened hand and palm in line with the mountain tops. She wrapped the fingers of her left hand tightly around her right wrist. "*Fulmen,*" Mirus called, her forearm glowing as a white crackle of lightning energy rippled from her palm toward the mountains, rocks exploding from the mountain tip in the distance and crumbling out of sight. "Now Derik, it's your turn."

Derik held the staff high, its point directed at the tip of the mountain. He closed his eyes and felt the energy surge within and around him. "*Fulmen.*" The energy surged from deep within, flowing from his chest, down his arm and through his hand and a bright blue spark exploded from the staff's crystal, hurling Derik backwards over the land's edge and toward the ocean below.

Mirus spun toward Derik, "*Mora Mōmentum.*" As the words left her lips a white light apparated beneath Derik's back, the force of the gravity pulling him toward the ocean beneath halting.

"*Contrārius.*" Mirus' mastery of her mana pulled Derik back up to the land's edge.

"Whoa. Thanks Mirus. That was close," Derik said, wiping his brow, I lost my footing."

"I did happen to notice that Derik. This is one of the three steps you need to learn before you bind with the staff. Balance. The second is reflex. I'm sure I will have some fun with that one. The third is connecting. You will need to connect your spirit, without fear, to the staff and show it your pure desires."

"What *fun* are you talking about Mirus? I mean, this first step almost sent me to the bottom of the ocean.

"Right. Come on Derik! One more time," Mirus' frustration showing in her wrinkled brow. "It's been hours and I am still being forced to catch you."

Derik regained his footing and once again held the staff high. "Ok Mirus. I will get it this time. I promise."

"I'm not going to catch you this time Derik. You need to ground yourself. Feel the energy in your body pull toward the ground and connect. If you fall this time, you fall," Mirus said, stepping back and turning to face her back to Derik.

'It's now or never,' Derik thought as he felt the energy begin to surge. "*Fulmen.*" A great crackle of blue lightning cracked over the mountain top in the distance, crumbling rocks falling beyond sight and Derik felt the surge down to his knees, flowing out his feet and into the earth below. The thrust pushed him gently backward, the dirt below grinding under his shoes.

"YOU DID IT!" Mirus said, already facing Derik, surprise clearly showing.

"I thought you were going to let me fall," Derik said, brushing his chest in triumph.

"Yes. I was. But the temptation of watching you fall was too great. I couldn't miss it," Mirus replied grinning. "I mean, it is a sight to see. The look of fear and disappointment in your face. Your feet leaving the ground. Haha."

Derik held the staff tightly and spun his body toward Mirus. "Well. I did it so are we going to move on to step two?"

Mirus simply shrugged. "Ok, Derik. This I have been looking forward to. We are going to go head-to-head."

"Wait...What?" Derik asked, knowing there is no hope he could beat Mirus.

"Don't worry Derik. I won't kill you. I mean all of Tellūs needs you. But as I said earlier. I won't be going easy on you. You need to learn how to gather your energy quickly."

Derik put his hands on his hips. "Alright Mirus. Let's go!"

Derik spun the staff around, the tip aimed at Mirus, and before he thought she could gain her ground he shot a zap of blue lightning toward her. Mirus slid to the side, using the stony ground to stop and kicked hard, flipping into the air and dodging the spark, before landing softly with ease.

"You are going to have to do better than that Derik."

"*Incendium.*" A bright red flame snaked toward Derik. He turned sharply, diving to the ground, the fiery blast singeing his sleeve as he rapidly regained his footing.

"*Navitas Pila,*" Derik called, a blue crackling ball making short work of the distance between the duo. Ducking, Mirus felt the energy ball lick her shoulder and during her lapse in concentration, Derik swiftly made up the ground between them and struck her chest with his foot, sending her to the ground. Derik jumped toward her, the force of his body landing on Mirus' chest knocking the wind out of her. He aimed the staff at her face and smiled wickedly.

"Well. I guess I now have my reflexes in check."

"Well done Derik. Next time when you're in this situation though," Mirus said pushing Derik off and getting to her feet, brushing the dirt from her sides. "Don't hesitate to finish.

The shadowed island of the Mystics began to fall over the ocean path in front of them as the sun began to set to the West.

"Alright Derik, it's now or never." Mirus turned to Derik, her hands clasped together. "You need to do this now. We must get across."

Derik held the staff high into the air and closed his eyes. His thoughts moulded into the face of his mother, Ranūl and all of Altāsia. His desire was to keep the memory of his mother alive, and that meant he needed to stay alive. Ranūl was his father, for no other words could rightfully explain their relationship. The people of Altāsia deserved to live without fear...he deserved to live without fear. Derik wrapped his fingers tightly around the staff. The energy he felt flowing through his body from the earth to his hands signalled it was time.

He thrust the staff downward, striking the ground hard. The staff shattered and the pieces floated in the air as if trapped within time itself before each part began to pierce Derik's arm one-by-one from his wrist to his elbow, a dark section of skin left behind following each strike. Derik fell to his knees. He felt no pain but it wasn't pleasant. The final piece floated into the air and struck his arm. Derik reached down and grabbed hold of his wrist, grunting as he felt a growing glow in his forearm.

He released his grip and watched as the darkened marks that had tainted his skin glowed a brilliant blue and faded to white.

"Alright, I think you are finally ready," Mirus smiled gently as she lead Derik to the ocean's edge. "Now, I need you to follow along *exactly*."

Mirus clasped her hands together. "Hands together, head down, concentrate. Feel the energy flowing from Tellūs beneath and then continue repeating the words *Tellūs Incrēmentum.*"

Both standing with their hands clasped together, heads down and eyes closed Derik and Mirus began whispering. "*Tellūs Incrēmentum.*"

A tearing, roaring noise broke from below them and the ground began to shake. Derik felt his stomach lurch but he fought the urge to turn and run, holding fast and continuing the incantation alongside Mirus. The ground cracked and juddered, the ocean below starting to bubble. Slowly, a line of linking, rounded stone columns emerged from the water reaching out to just a few inches above the surface. They stretched out as far as the island, creating a pathway of stepping stones which would take them across the sea and straight to the Valley of Mystics.

Mirus opened her eyes and took hold of Derik's hand. "Ready?" she asked. Derik took a deep breath and nodded. Mirus let go of his hand and took the first steps onto the stone causeway.

CHAPTER 14
THE RELEASE

His heart pounded in his chest with every leap closer to the isle of the Valley of Mystics and Derik could feel the fear of knowing what lay ahead creep deep into his very being. Even with the extra strength he now possessed through the energies flooding his body, he was desperately worried and it was written all over his face.

"Mirus, what if we don't beat Elanore?" he said finally expressing the thought that had been lingering at the back of his mind. "I mean, if we can't stop her, what happens then?"

"I don't like to think about what *might* happen, Derik. I try to focus on what I *will* to happen," Mirus replied, wobbling a little as her feet plopped flat onto the next stepping stone.

Derik smiled to himself. He was now used to her witty remarks. They were growing on him and he had learned to expect no less from her.

"Have you noticed the clouds?" he said, gesturing toward the growing swirl of black clouds hovering above the Valley of Mystics.

"I have! They seem to be building in strength the closer we get to the island," she replied, slipping the half Mystic Stone from her pocket and rolling it in her palm. "The other half must be close and Elanore's energy knows it," she added, slipping it safely back and looking to Derik, who had stopped short and was staring at the shore behind her.

"Derik?" she said questionably, spinning on her heels to follow his stare. "Huh!? It's a Barque. It seems Xardos and his goons got here the easy way!" she said smugly, crossing her arms as they both stared at the long wooden boat docked along the shoreline.

Derik's forehead creased with frustration. "Xardos. Now there is a sorry excuse for an existence!" The pressure from his tightly balled fists had turned his knuckles white, his nails digging into his palms.

"Xardos...he's that goon we had the misfortune of meeting in the Regius Ranges. *He* has the other half of the stone?" Mirus' question came across as pure surprise.

"Yeah and I bet he's expecting us," Derik replied. "Mirus, please tell me there is more than one way into the valley than the opening in front of us?"

"Well. There is a secret entrance," she whispered. "Argonus used it to enter undetected when Elanore and her army of Mystics were taking rest from battle here. Not many people know of the true story. How Elanore came so close to her conquest and how my great grandfather ensnared her. We should be safe getting in through there.

As they neared the outer Northern edge of the valley, the clouds above began to crackle with flashes of purple lightning, reaching through the skies like veins. The air felt heavy and damp against Derik's face and he was glad when Mirus suddenly stopped and leaned against the moss covered wall to the valley. Derik wiped the perspiration building on his face, straining to hear the enchantment sneaking from Mirus' lips. She lifted her face, eyes widened with concentration as pure streams of light penetrated outward from the rock leaving Derik's sight in a haze. He rubbed his eyes, blinking them in desperation as slowly the blur faded and he was left facing an opening to a dark cavern.

Only the sounds of their footsteps and the thundering noises coming from above could be heard as the duo made their way carefully through the cavern. Mirus nudged Derik's arm gently after a few short steps and mouthed for him to '*be ready*' to which he nodded sharply and began to focus his inner energies while they made their way deeper.

The entrance to the other end of the cavern came into view as flashes of light from the storm above blinked onto the walls.

Mirus stopped suddenly spinning to catch hold of Derik's arm.

"Derik. I need to say something before we...well I'm not actually sure what is about to happen," she said, staring deeply into his eyes. "Actually that is exactly what I wanted to talk about."

Her grip tightened on his arm and Derik turned his complete attention to the now very serious looking Mirus.

"I'm not sure what we are about to step into. And I don't like walking blind. I guess... I just wanted to say be careful and thank you." With her last words Mirus lowered her eyes to the floor. Derik took a step toward her and reached out his hand, putting it to her chin and raising her head until she was once again looking into his eyes.

"We can win this! I mean once Elanore is released, we just need to..." Derik's words fell silent as a series of loud howls interrupted, bouncing off the walls around them. In the few seconds it took Mirus and Derik to realise what was happening, four shadows emerged from behind a boulder fixed to the side of the entrance beside them, one knocking Derik to the sandy floor and another moving swiftly to take hold of Mirus, gripping her tightly by the shoulders. Derik struggled to his feet, a pressure wrapping around his throat as he was lifted into the air by one of the shadows. Mirus struggled at the muscular arms holding her in place, hissing and spitting as she tried to scratch and kick her way free from the goon's clutches.

"How sweet of an exchange that was between you two. One would almost think you...well, not that any of that matters now that you have *finally* arrived." The deep voice coming from a tall thin man emerging from the shadows in front of them. Easily recognising the voice, Derik stopped struggling for just long enough to see a smirking Xardos waltz slowly to Mirus' side, ripping her dress and reaching into her pocket, snatching the second half of the Mystic Stone.

"NOOO!" she screamed in desperation, but it was too late. Xardos held the stone high in the air with his left hand and then raised his right, holding tightly the other half of the stone. A short moment of total silence lingered, before with a roar of triumph Xardos joined the two halves together.

A deafening boom vibrated through the very air around the group huddled just outside the cavern entrance and the valley begun to flood with a dense swirling black smoke, fading apart to illuminate the figure of Elanore bursting free from her stone prison. She held her head back and screeched into the sky like a wild Regius, disappearing as the smoke engulfed her once more.

"What are you doing?" screamed Mirus at an awe-struck Xardos, his eyes glassy and fixed in a trance toward the clouds. She looked in desperation at Derik, whose face reflected her own horror. The two Halflings had released their grip awe stricken as much as their superior, but Derik and Mirus stood rooted to the spot.

A green flash broke through the dark clouding revealing the grand enchanter; a free Elanore. Vanishing swiftly from sight she reappeared mid-air above the group, a wicked smile stretching the width of her face.

"And so, it begins!" whispered Mirus hoarsely to Derik, a look of determination his silent response.

With a graceless cry, Xardos fell to his knees. "Oh my lady," he said. "At last you have returned to us. I have released you! Yes it was I who saved you my Elanore, my Queen. Together we can rule Altāsia. Together we can once more make this land great and..."

"SILENCE!" screamed the sorceress, extending her long pointed index finger toward the blundering man. A painful scream ripped from his throat and Xardos exploded into a purple mist, leaving nothing but a dark mark where he had been kneeling. His three goons stood in shock as their superior was reduced to nothing before them, suddenly scrambling, pushing each other out of the way in their race to escape the valley.

Mirus had not drifted her gaze from Elanore and at last the wicked enchanter turned her attention to her and smirked.

"I know you! Ha, a descendant of Argonus? You stink of the same spirit!" She spat, her voice cutting through the air like an icy dagger.

"You shall not succeed, Elanore," replied Mirus. "I will destroy you. And be it forever."

"You?" patronised the enchanter. "You?" And she let out a long cackle of laughter.

Derik watched horrified, as incandescent with rage Mirus raised her hand, firing a blast of pure white swirling energy towards Elanore. A cloud of blinding light enclosed the great enchanter as the power bolt hit its target, but in the rapidly clearing smoke Elanore was revealed unscathed and still hovering above them without even a tear in her long, dark, draping dress.

"As you can see, I've had a little time to learn a few new tricks since I've been ... otherwise occupied," she laughed shrilly. Derik and Mirus again began to feel the air around them building with vibrations. Their skin tingled and prickled as Elanore began drawing power from the very earth surrounding them, the ground beneath crumbling and falling into deep chasms of boiling pools of lava opening up all throughout the valley.

"I am immortal now," Elanore smiled widely with pleasure.

"We'll see about that!" cried Mirus darting past Elanore and beckoning for Derik to follow her lead.

The duo took turns firing blasts of white and blue crackling energy toward Elanore as they dashed through the valley, taking shelter from the returned fire of dark purple streaks Elanore sparked toward the two with ease.

Derik dodged another purple blast, leaping for the ground, rolling and springing to his feet to face the enchanter. He raised his arm, but the fear trembling through his body seem to take affect and he couldn't feel the energy surge. Elanore sneered, and in a flash of purple mana she was standing beside Derik. With a powerful flick he was lifted off his feet and slammed into a nearby tree, landing heavily with a grunt of pain. He pulled himself to his feet, leaning against the tree for balance and held his aching abdomen.

"And now you!" screamed the dark sorceress spinning around to direct a flash of sparks at Mirus, knocking her to the ground and sending her sliding towards one of the crumbling fiery pits that were scattered across the valley.

"MIRUS!" shouted Derik, gritting his teeth against the pain shooting through his left side. He ran towards her, catching hold of her arm as she slipped down the steaming crevasse in the earth. His muscles burned with pain and every ligament stretched almost to breaking point as he struggled to hold on to Mirus. Derik pulled again with all the strength he could muster and Mirus grabbed the crumbling outer edges, the duo straining as Mirus crawled back to safety.

"Not so fast!" Elanore's shrill warning was backed as she extended her thin arm and blasted a ball of purple mana at Mirus. As it struck her the ball expanded, encapsulating Mirus within. She looked longingly to Derik. He looked back into her eyes and for a brief instant neither spoke, time seeming to understand the moment. "This is your destiny. You must defeat her," she whispered, her face calm and determined. A shrill scream of dark delight came from behind Derik as Elanore pushed the sphere back down, deep into the pit.

"NOO…MIRUS!" cried Derik, staring through the thick clouds of sulphur rising from the hole, but another blast from Elanore threw him to the side, painfully reminding him of the task he still had to complete.

Derik's body convulsed with pain and his mind was in anguish as he grieved the loss of Mirus. With a growling snarl he released a shimmering bolt of energy at Elanore, this time finding its mark. A squeal of anger ripped from her lips and Elanore returned fire blasting the rock beside him into pebbles that rose and rained from the sky above.

Derik covered his head straining through the dust shrouding his vision when a sudden purple flash struck his leg, the pain and the exhaustion overcoming him. He sank to the ground as Elanore swooped overhead cackling with pleasure.

"Say goodbye BOY. Your end has come," she hissed at him. "Pity. Such a waste of powerful life."

She lifted her arm to strike and a slight sense of relief washed through Derik's tired body as he closed his eyes and waited, prepared for death. The initial strike was agonising as he squirmed, his mind racing with thoughts of his mother, Ranūl and the people of Tellūs he had let down. But the pain didn't last. A scream of power again rippled through the valley surrounding them before falling silent. Derik mustered the strength to creak open an eye and was surprised to see Elanore lying on the ground struggling against an array of light-stricken arrows zipping through the air.

Derik drudged to his feet, his hope beginning to restore as Ilaseon and an army of Light Workers fired sets of arrows from the rocky tips of the valley's edge.

Ilaseon threw down his bow and unsheathed a sword from his side, signalling for the front group to charge the valley, while streaks of light zipped over their heads from the remaining Light Workers perched along the rocky tips.

Pulling arrows from her thigh with a flick of her hand, Elanore got to her feet and swiftly soared into the air, dodging the next set of arrows that had been cast toward her. She lifted both hands and blasted a crackling ball of energy at the group of arrow men, a sprinkling of screams bringing back her wicked smile as several Light Workers fell to the smoking earth.

"You're making me angry…no more playing. *EXERIOR MYSTICUS!*" she screamed. Through a great bellowing ocean of swirling smoke, an army of Mystics swarmed into the valley. Their large wings stretched out as each took off toward the group of charging Light Workers, almost knocking Derik to his feet as they sailed passed. Elanore turned her attention toward Ilaseon, as he dodged through the army of Mystics, gaining ground to within striking distance of the dark enchanter.

Ilaseon lunged toward her. As swift as lightning Elanore raised a hand and sent him hurtling toward the ground, caught in a sheet of purple sparks. She lifted her head and laughed a shrill snort of triumph, while her army systematically continued to attack each charging group of Light Workers; great fiery streams engulfing Ilaseon's brotheren one-by-one.

More Light Workers began to appear over the valley's edge and it seemed their numbers would never be exhausted, even though Derik could see they were dying in their hundreds. Elanore's attention was occupied by the attacks and as she strained to control her army as well as the lunging attacks of Ilaseon, Derik knew he had one chance, and this was it.

'*What would Mirus do?*' he thought as an image of her appeared in his mind.

Mimicking an elegant, power pose that Mirus would be proud of, he put his hands together, index fingers pointed towards the sky and then as if he had known it his whole life, the incantation that Argonus had used to ensnare Elanore within the stone roared from his lips.

"*Lapis Intra Laqueus!*"

Caught off guard, Elanore was frozen in the act of sending another energy volt towards Ilaseon. As Derik watched, scarcely able to believe his eyes, the enchanter quickly became ensnared in a rising pool of liquid stone, moving from her feet engulfing her body and solidifying as it went.

Summoning the last hint of energy in his body, Derik screamed at the top of his lungs and a dazzling sheet of bright blue fired from his body towards the stone-encased enchanter, sending her into a nearby lava pit, obliterating the centuries old enchanter in a spectacular cloud of black and green smoke.

Falling to the ground through exhaustion, Derik dragged himself to Ilaseon who was lying on the ground badly burned, but alive. Derik reached out a hand toward his pack, which lay across the valley against a tree and concentrated. His mana built deep inside and he connected with his pack, summoning it through the air and to his side. He reached in and removed the full bottle of Phoenix tears, popping the cork top and dripping the liquid over the wounded Light Workers. Derik sat watching as each coat of broken skin etched itself back together, handing the bottle to Ilaseon as he sat up and looked around at his fallen comrades.

In a moment of sheer hope, Derik raced over to the pit Mirus had fallen down, but the pit only contained the bubbling sulphurous liquid gurgling far below.

Tears rolled down his face and he got to his feet, closing his eyes in respect of the fallen heroin.

"We did it Mirus!" Derik whispered.

Ilaseon held a hand up to silence the healed and now chattering Light Workers.

"Derik, you have saved all our lives through your bravery and wilfulness to never relinquishing hope. An unbreakable bond has been forged between us," he said. "This will last until the end of time, for we are now Brotheren."

Derik nodded. "Thank you Ilaseon, we are indeed Brotheren," he said placing a hand on the Keeper of Light's shoulder.

"We are all sorry more than words can say, about the loss of your friend, our sister, Mirus," continued Ilaseon. "But now the time has come for us to leave as our forest home awaits. We would advise you too to return home, for your duty here is done."

Derik stood thinking about his journey. From the moment he left home in Lūnam he'd never thought he would become more than just a 'traveller,' as his mother would say, and he knew that Ilaseon was right. Although it almost broke his heart to do so, he would have to leave Mirus where she had been laid to rest.

As the Light Workers began to make their way back through the valley, Derik picked up his pack and with a final salute to Ilaseon, and a lingering look at the pit where Mirus had vanished, he set off for Lūnam, a slight smile forming at the thought of home.

ABOUT DAVID JAMES

It was at a young age that David James found his love for the written word. He enjoyed sitting quietly and reading a range of genres with his favourites including history and science-fiction.

At age 14, he found his passion for writing and began penning the Altāsia Legends series.

David published his first illustrated children's book, 'Calm of the Storm,' in 2019, followed by 'Light in the Dark' in 2020.

Today, David still enjoys reading history and science-fiction, but has gained a passion for true crime and thrillers.

www.ingramcontent.com/pod-product-compliance
Lightning Source LLC
Chambersburg PA
CBHW060819310726
48980CB00002B/347

* 9 7 8 0 6 4 8 9 6 0 1 1 9 *